All of Tinsley Cove would be watching.

Maybe they should come up with a plan that would give them the on-screen drama he needed for the show but also allow them to keep their dignity.

Logan asked, "What are you thinking?"

"This." Cassie leaned in and pressed her lips to his.

For the span of a heartbeat, Logan was disoriented as if the axis of his world had tipped and left him hanging upside down.

A voice in his head said, "Stop. You shouldn't be doing this." But his body was singing another tune. As Cassie opened her mouth to deepen the kiss, his nerve endings sizzled like live wires, making his body vibrate until he couldn't hear anything over the need rushing through his veins.

He pulled her tighter and leaned into the kiss as if his breathing depended on it.

The next thing he knew, she'd pulled back slightly. Still holding on to him, she stared up at him dreamily.

"I was thinking we should get that out of the way so we can move on with what we need to do," she said. "It wasn't so bad, was it?"

Dear Reader,

The beginning of a new series is exhilarating and a little daunting. It's a blank canvas where anything can happen. When I was sketching out the idea for Tinsley Cove, I drew on several things.

First, when I was growing up, the beach was my playground. It still speaks to my soul, and lately, I've had a yearning for the sand, the salt water and the roar of the wind in my ears. Second, I have a thing for real estate and interior design shows. I can't get enough of them. The third factor was my Pembroke Welsh corgi, Luna. She's a bundle of energy and sweetness and she always listens when I talk. Of course she does—there might be a treat involved.

I mixed up these colorful ideas, threw them at the canvas and voilà! The McFaddens of Tinsley Cove.

Cassie and Logan kick off the series. I hope you'll enjoy their story as much as I loved writing it. Please keep in touch. I love to hear from readers.

NancyRobardsThompson.com

Instagram.com/NancyRThompson

Facebook.com/NRobardsThompson

Warmly,

Nancy

Selling Sandcastle

NANCY ROBARDS THOMPSON

HARLEQUIN
SPECIAL
EDITION

HARLEQUIN®
SPECIAL
EDITION™

Recycling programs for this product may not exist in your area.

ISBN-13: 978-1-335-72444-1

Selling Sandcastle

Copyright © 2023 by Nancy Robards Thompson

For questions and comments about the quality of this book, please contact us at CustomerService@Harlequin.com.

Harlequin Enterprises ULC
22 Adelaide St. West, 41st Floor
Toronto, Ontario M5H 4E3, Canada
www.Harlequin.com

Printed in U.S.A.

Nationally bestselling author **Nancy Robards Thompson** holds a degree in journalism. She worked as a newspaper reporter until she realized reporting "just the facts" bored her silly. Now that she has much more content to report to her muse, Nancy loves writing women's fiction and romance full-time. Critics have deemed her work "funny, smart and observant." She resides in Florida with her husband and daughter. You can reach her at Facebook.com/nrobardsthompson.

Visit the Author Profile page
at Harlequin.com for more titles.

This book is dedicated to my Pembroke Welsh corgi, Luna, who is every bit as sweet and sassy as she appears in this book.

Chapter One

Cassie Houston turned around in a circle and surveyed the skyline of moving boxes covering the walls of her brand-new living room.

"Where could that dress be?" she said. "You were supposed to help me stay organized, Luna."

The corgi tilted her head to the side as if trying her best to understand the question.

Cassie wasn't blaming the little dog, of course. Having conversations with her pup had become as natural as talking to herself. Over the years, the animal had proved to be a better listener than her ex-husband and was certainly more empathetic, which was part of the reason why he was her *ex*-husband.

Luna crouched with her front paws on the ground

and her cute little behind up in the air. Her nub of a tail wagged as she let out a sound that registered somewhere between a yowl and a yodel.

The reaction always made Cassie smile. She bent down and scratched the sweet red sable dog behind her velvety ears.

"I know it's not your fault, lovie, but I need to find that bag fast or I'll be late for my first day. They'll fire me before I even start."

In a whirlwind of change, Cassie had moved from central Florida to the small beach town of Tinsley Cove, North Carolina, to join the cast of a scripted reality show.

On a whim, she and her sister, Gabriella, had attended an open audition for an amateur cooking competition show at Universal Studios in Orlando. It wasn't really Cassie's idea of a fun way to kill a Saturday, but since her divorce more than a year and a half ago, she'd been trying to keep an open mind about new experiences. Plus, Gabby, who was always up for anything, had promised to pay for lunch if Cassie would go with her. So, the two of them ventured to the theme park to try out.

Cassie had no illusions. What were the chances of a twenty-seven-year-old amateur being plucked from obscurity to be a contestant on a competition for home cooks? Especially when the line for the audition nearly stretched around the park and the best thing she'd ever made for dinner was reservations.

Even so, she was spending time with her sister. That still felt like a luxury. Cassie's ex, Troy, had been selectively possessive, meaning that anytime she wanted to spend time with her sister, he balked. He was convinced Gabby didn't like him. In hindsight, it was true. Troy had never been particularly cordial to Gabby, and in the last year of their marriage, he'd been downright callous. Could you blame her?

The audition line had moved surprisingly fast. When it was her turn, all she'd had to do was fill out an application, allow them to take a photograph of her and introduce herself to the camera, stating her name, her hometown and one unique fact about herself.

The unique fact had caught her by surprise. All she could think to say was that she was a shopaholic, but at the last minute she'd tossed in, "I guess you could say I'm a princess. I used to be married to the son of the Central Florida Furniture King, which makes him the Central Florida Furniture Prince?"

It had slipped out.

The minute the words had leaped from her mouth, she'd cringed, but the casting team had laughed. Dalton Hart, the honcho of Top Drawer Productions, said, "Your royal highness, it's a pleasure to meet you. You're a breath of fresh air."

He was slick and self-assured in the way most Hollywood producers were—though, full disclosure, she'd never met an actual producer...from Hollywood or otherwise. In fact, she didn't even know if Dalton and company were from Hollywood. Though his golden-streaked hair and Tom Cruise smile made him look as if he'd fallen right from the city of angels.

When he'd handed her his business card, she'd gotten her hopes up for about three seconds, but when she'd walked out of the audition, past the long line of people who were still waiting, the balloon popped and she'd landed in reality with a solid thud.

While she was trying to stay open to new adventures such as going to the open casting, her divorce had taught her to stay firmly grounded . Denying the truth when it was in front of her face didn't change the facts.

But, hey, even if the audition ended up being a bust, it was totally worth it. She'd enjoyed a fun day with her sister. She'd spent time with someone who loved her, someone who wanted to be with her, and that was more than enough.

Imagine her surprise when, three weeks later, she got a call from a California area code. Of course, she let it sail over to voice mail. She didn't know anyone from the West Coast, but after the caller left a message, she listened to it.

"Hi, I'm calling for Cassie Houston. This is Dalton Hart from Top Drawer Productions. We met when you auditioned for *Cooking from the Hart*, one of the competition shows my company produces. Unfortunately, you weren't selected as a contestant for *Cooking*, but I may have another opportunity for you. Would you please give me a call as soon as possible?"

At first, she thought Gabby was playing some kind of elaborate prank on her, but then she dug out Dalton Hart's business card…and the number matched.

He told her he was producing another reality show—not a competition, but more of a lightly scripted show centered around North Carolina luxury real estate, and he thought she would be a perfect fit.

"This is unexpected," she'd said. "The only problem is I've never sold real estate in North Carolina—or anywhere else, for that matter."

"That is not a problem. I have a note here on your *Cooking* audition form that says you worked in furniture. Is that right?"

Sort of…

"My ex-husband's family owns a furniture store. I did…*um*…interior decorating for them."

The Central Florida Furniture King was regionally famous for its scratch-and-dent furnishings. Cassie had staged various pieces into makeshift rooms so the customers could see that even though the goods were lightly damaged, they could still work. When strategically placed, you'd never know the sofa had a big gash where a careless warehouse worker had slashed it with a box cutter or a nasty stain of unknown origin.

"Fantastic," Dalton said. "That's exactly what we're looking for—someone with an eye for style who can stage a room."

He was a bit cryptic about the details, other than he and his production team would record the pilot very soon, and it would air on primetime TV. Once they had solidified the cast and nailed down the details, the PR team would make announcements.

Over the course of a few more phone calls and one signed nondisclosure agreement, she learned accepting the offer would involve a move to Tinsley Cove, North Carolina. She'd never heard of the place, but okay…that's what the internet was for.

It also meant she'd have to quit her job.

After she and Troy had broken up, she'd given up her position at the family's furniture store. They didn't exactly fire her, but it was abundantly clear that it would've been awkward if she'd stayed out of principle. Cassie had tried to find the silver lining. Furniture had never really been her calling. This was a chance to branch out and do something fun for a change…like work in fashion, or even sell real estate.

It was ironic when the only job she could find was in the furniture department at a department store in the mall. It paid the bills, and she promised herself she'd keep looking for something else, but funny how it felt like she'd blinked and almost two years had gone by.

This was a sign from the universe that it was time to move on…even if she would still be working with furniture.

Dalton had underscored that, until further notice, the location was top secret. He all but threatened an evil curse on her life if she blabbed and word got out.

"Yes, the nondisclosure I signed made that perfectly clear," she'd said.

"That's the kind of humor I'm looking for," he'd said. "I'm counting on you to bring that kind of sassy drama. Can you do it, Cassie?"

"Of course, Dalton."

While Cassie had never thought of herself as a drama queen, drama certainly had defined her life for the past several years.

She hadn't gone into that with Dalton. Not even after he said, "When you introduced yourself as a princess because you'd been married to the Furniture King—" She hadn't corrected him – Troy's father was the king. Her ex was the crown prince- even though it was tempting to dish about the Furniture King's outrageous television commercials, which starred her ex-husband. Troy had prided himself on being the face of his father's company and ate it up when someone recognized him out in the wild. As if he were Brad Pitt and not a buffoon who wore a plastic crown, red onesie and a matching fake fur-trimmed velvet cape while he hopped from one piece of furniture to another and shouted, "If you don't buy from the Central Florida Furniture King, you must be the village idiot."

And that, ladies and gentlemen, that was the man she had promised to love until death tore the marriage asunder. Or, in their case, until she'd discovered he was a lying, cheating scumbag.

"After you made us laugh, I couldn't forget you," Dalton had continued. "The whole team felt the same way. You were like a breath of fresh air, but with a definite *oh, no, she didn't just say that* kind of vibe. And that's the feel we want you to bring to the Tinsley Cove show. Just be yourself, Cassie. Can you do that? *Huh? Huh?*"

Despite the ugly voice that screamed *being yourself wasn't good enough for Troy or his family*, she heard herself squeaking, "Being myself is what I do best."

She had to be herself. That was all she had left.

After their final conversation, everything had happened so fast. She'd only had a week to pack and move, because they needed her in Tinsley Cove ASAP.

The salary seemed generous enough, and it even included housing for three months. Filming would take about ten weeks, and then they wanted her to stick close during the postproduction process, until they were sure they had all the footage they needed.

After Cassie gave a verbal confirmation that she was onboard, Dalton's assistant had emailed her a contract, which she'd returned the next day.

She was allowed to tell her sister the premise of the show: it followed a family-owned real estate agency that sold luxury beachfront properties in North Carolina.

But she and Gabby had to keep everything on the down low until the official announcement went out to the media.

Finally, today was the day that she would get the rest of the scoop.

Her stomach fluttered as the reality that she was going to be on TV—on *national television*—set in.

She would meet the family today at the first official production meeting. In the meantime, she was not to tell anyone in Tinsley Cove why she was here—not the guy at the gas station where she'd filled up her car. Not the nice server she'd met at the restaurant where she'd grabbed a quick dinner last night. Not even Sophie, the property manager who had given her the keys to the tiny bungalow she'd be living in for the next three months.

All this hush-hush, top secret vaguery would end soon.

Now, if she could only find her missing dress and not have a panic attack in the process.

Even though she had plenty of other clothes to

choose from, wearing that particular floral-print Alice + Olivia today felt important.

New dress plus new job…on national television… Her heart hammered.

Stop freaking yourself out!

She cleared her throat and said out loud, "New dress plus new job equals new start."

It had to be around here somewhere. She'd put it in a black garment bag, which was supposed to have been packed in her car.

Now, the car was empty, and the bag was nowhere to be found. The only thing that made sense was that maybe Gabby, who had graciously helped her pack, had misunderstood and had mistakenly packed it in one of the many wardrobe boxes along with the rest of her clothes.

But which one?

She tapped her chin with her finger as she turned in a circle, trying to decide where to look next. There were a lot of wardrobe boxes. *A lot.* Clothes were her weakness. She wasn't embarrassed to admit it. People had worse vices, she reasoned as she pulled the packing tape off one of the boxes the movers had deposited in the living room.

Maybe bringing every piece of clothing she owned had been excessive? True, Dalton had said this was not a big-budget operation. There was no money for wardrobe and makeup, but what would Dalton do if she asked him if she could trade the housing cost for a wardrobe allowance, hair stylist and makeup artist?

She knew what he'd do—he'd laugh and tell her to channel that spirit into the show.

She sat down on the couch with a hard thud. What if the show edited her to look like a diva? Shows did that sometimes. Spirit was one thing, but *diva-ness* was completely not what she was about.

Oh, God. Is it too late to back out?

Cassie shook the thought away as she lifted the box's flap and peered inside. There was no sign of the black garment bag. Only a selection of winter wear— coats, suits and dresses, none of which would be appropriate for this humid June morning. Of course, she'd hardly worn any of them in Florida, but each piece was so beautiful she hadn't been able to resist adding them to her collection. There was always the chance that she'd travel somewhere cold.

Okay, so that was a stretch, but a girl could dream. She brushed the soft sleeve of a cashmere sweater across her cheek and heard her sister, Gabby, rubbing in the fact that Cassie should've had her own savings account. That she should've put away the money rather than squandering it on clothes. If she had, she might have a down payment for a house.

Cassie had countered that those weren't the things a woman thinks about when she's young and in love. It would be like betting against the marriage. But how was Gabby to know that since she'd never been married?

Cassie sighed and swiped her hand across her damp forehead. It was so warm in the house. The cashmeres made her feel like she was about to suffocate. Letting the box lid fall closed, she got up to check the thermostat again.

The missing-dress crisis wasn't the only thing making her sweat. The temperature in the house had climbed to seventy-nine. It was two degrees warmer since she'd gotten out of the shower this morning. Now, her pink terry bathrobe was only trapping the heat. She moved the robe's fluffy lapels back and forth trying to cool herself off, but it only moved warm air.

She thought about calling Sophie and reminding her to send someone over to have a look at the HVAC unit. Last night, while she was showing Cassie around, her landlord had mentioned that the air seemed a little stagnant. She'd promised to have someone look at it. Cassie had to trust that Sophie would follow through.

In the meantime, Cassie untied her robe and let it fall to the floor, leaving her in her bra and panties as she opened the remaining boxes in the living room.

She'd lived in Florida all her life, never making more than a cross-town move. She'd sorely underestimated the enormity of a move to a new state. She could've used more time to get organized.

She'd accepted the job on Monday. On Saturday, the moving truck rolled up ready to pack her belongings. Yesterday, she'd awakened at the crack of dawn and herded Luna into the car, which was packed with her most important possessions, and she'd made the nine-hour drive from Orlando to Tinsley Cove.

After Sophie, who lived next door, had handed off the keys, Cassie had directed where the movers should deposit the furniture and boxes.

When it started storming, the organized move-in turned to chaos. The movers ran in and out, tracking up the wooden floors as they deposited the soggy boxes in the first space they could find.

By the time Cassie had signed off on the move, she'd been utterly exhausted and homesick, second-guessing whether she'd made the right decision to accept this job. It felt like Mother Nature was crying all the unshed tears that Cassie had bottled up inside herself since the day Troy had blindsided her with the news that he wanted a divorce.

She chalked it up to being hungry and tired – and hot. After grabbing a quick bite, she'd fallen into bed determined to get a good night's sleep.

Around 4:00 a.m., she'd awakened with a start, realizing the black bag that contained her new dress hadn't been among the things she'd unpacked from the car. She'd tossed and turned, acutely aware of the heat and humidity—and the house's every creak, moan and sigh. Finally, she'd gotten up to search for the dress, and she'd been awake ever since.

Now, the morning dawned sunny and bright—and even hotter, if that was possible. Even so, the way the sun streamed in through the living room window seemed as if it was offering a promise that everything would be okay.

She would put on her new dress and wow everyone with her sass and style.

When Troy eventually saw the show he would eat his heart out.

Of course, before she could wow anyone, she needed to find that garment bag… It had to be in one of the boxes. Maybe Gabby remembered which one she'd put it in?

Cassie made her way into the kitchen, scooped up her phone off the marble island and dialed her sister's number.

The phone rang three times. Just as Cassie was about to hang up, Gabby picked up and croaked, "Do you know what time it is?"

"Good morning to you, too," Cassie said. "Yes, I'm very aware of the time, because I'm afraid I'm going to be late on my first day."

"If you're in such a hurry, why are you calling me?"

"Gabby, what did you do with that black garment bag that had my new Alice + Olivia dress in it?"

"What? I don't know."

"Remember, I asked you to put it in my car when you were carrying out my suitcases. It wasn't in the car. Do you remember if you packed it in one of the wardrobe boxes that was going on the moving truck?"

Her sister was quiet for a moment.

"*Um…* I don't remember. I'm sorry, I don't re-member you telling me to take the hanging bag to the car."

Cassie sighed. "That's okay. Everything was mov-ing kind of fast."

"I know, right?" Gabby said. "I'm sorry for the mix-up. Have a great day and call me later to let me know how everything goes, okay?"

"I will. Miss you, Gabs. Bye."

After Cassie disconnected the call, the back of her throat ached and her eyes stung.

Even if this day wasn't off to the most auspicious start, with a broken AC and a missing dress, she wasn't going to let it derail her.

She had plenty of other things to wear.

In one of the boxes in her bedroom, she'd spied the pair of cropped white Kate Spade pants – the ones with the bow at the waist. She'd pair them with her sleeveless hot pink ruffle top…as long as it didn't need to be ironed. There wasn't time for that. Plus, she hadn't found the iron yet.

Had she even brought the iron?

That's why she needed to find the floral dress,

but it looked like that wasn't going to happen. She'd looked through just about every wardrobe box in the house. The only place she hadn't looked was the garage. The movers had put most of the boxes in the house, and there had been plenty of room to pull her car into the garage, but still she thought she remembered seeing a few boxes out there.

Hand on the doorknob, Cassie thought about putting on her robe, but the windowless garage was completely private. In this heat, her robe would feel like a parka. Even the mere thought of it caused beads of perspiration to form on her forehead.

She flipped on the garage light, and the door closed behind her. The dank space smelled of damp concrete, soggy cardboard and fresh paint.

Her car took up most of the room, but a thirty-five-pound sack of Luna's dog food sat propped against the wall next to the door, right where she'd left it. Six small boxes were pushed against the far wall on the other side of the car.

Three were labeled *Books*. Two were labeled *Kitchen*. One was labeled *Miscellaneous Garage*. Cassie's heart sank when she realized they were all too small to be wardrobe boxes.

Clearly, the dress wasn't in the garage, either. It was as if it had vanished into thin air.

She sighed. Her plan B outfit—the cropped white Kate Spade pants and an unwrinkled blouse—would have to be today's good-luck charm.

Cassie twisted the knob of the door that led back into the house, but it didn't budge. She tried again, this time cranking it harder and giving a little shoulder shove to the door.

It didn't move.

"Are you kidding me?"

She pounded on the door, and Luna barked in response. Panic seared through her as she remembered too late Sophie's warning yesterday—the door going out to the garage had an automatic locking mechanism. "It might feel like it's unlocked when you twist the knob on the inside," Sophie had said, "but make sure the lock is vertical before you step out. If it closes with the turn button parallel to the floor, you'll lock yourself out. It needs to be pointing up and down or you'll need a key to let yourself in."

Cassie's hands flew to her mouth, and she cursed under her breath.

She had locked herself out.

Chapter Two

"This cannot be happening," Cassie cried out as she tried the handle again.

Oh, but it is.

"Why would anyone put an automatic lock on a door? That's just asking for trouble."

Her words seemed to mock her as they bounced off the garage's concrete walls.

Now, she'd have to go next door and ask Sophie to let her in. She was definitely going to be late and—

She gasped as the real predicament hit her. Not only was she locked out of her house…but she was wearing nothing but her underwear.

Unless she wanted to run next door half-naked in broad daylight, she needed to figure something out fast.

She glanced around for something—anything—she could toss on to cover herself—a tarp, a furniture blanket the movers might have left behind. But there was nothing.

She didn't even have a cell phone to call Dalton to give him the heads-up that she was going to be late for her first day because she was…locked out of her house in her undies.

Frantically, she tore open the small boxes. The books and kitchen knife set and appliances were no help. The All-Clad cookware set that had belonged to her mother wouldn't work—she couldn't very well go next door with two pots and a lid covering her lady parts. She upended the box labeled Garage. The contents of a tool kit, a power drill and an assortment of picture-hanging hardware spilled out.

Maybe she could use the drill to remove the doorknob.

Nope.

On closer inspection, there were no visible screws to unscrew. She was a lot of things, but she wasn't mechanical, and now wasn't the time to try and learn.

Cassie was on the verge of a panic attack when inspiration struck. Maybe she could fashion one of the boxes into a sandwich board type of cover?

She tried, but in the end, the boxes were too small. People would still be able to see her underwear from the sides…but if it was all she had to work with, maybe it was better than nothing, because she couldn't stay in the garage indefinitely. Maybe she could cut one of the boxes at the seam and wrap it around her like a beach towel?

Then her gaze landed on the big bag of dog food. *Even better.*

She grabbed a knife from the set and carefully cut open the top of the dog-food bag. After emptying the contents into one of the boxes that she hadn't cut up, she sliced the bag down the middle, then cut two armholes in the sides.

She slipped on her bespoke minidress and fashioned a piece of picture-hanging wire around her waist as a belt. It wasn't ideal, but at least she wouldn't give the neighborhood a peep show.

After one last check to make sure all her girl parts were covered, she took a deep breath and pushed the button of the automatic garage door opener and hurried across the lush, green side lawn that stretched between her house and Sophie's place. The sun shone bright in the clear blue sky. Cassie hesitated a moment when she saw the truck in Sophie's driveway. It wasn't her neighbor's. Yesterday, Sophie was driving a silver Prius. This vehicle was a shiny black truck.

Darn, that meant Sophie had company. Clearly, this wasn't a good time to prevail upon her landlord, but since she was locked out, she really didn't have a choice. All Cassie could do was hope that Sophie would understand.

Maybe the truck didn't belong to a guy. Women drove trucks. Maybe one of Sophie's friends had stopped by for breakfast.

Wouldn't it be funny if the three of them bonded over this crazy situation? What a way to make friends, but yes, Cassie could totally see it happening. They'd laugh at how Cassie had landed on Sophie's front porch wearing, of all things, a dog food–bag dress. They'd joke about wanting to borrow it— No, better yet, they'd say, "Cassie, design a dress for me. You're so creative—you're starting a whole new trend."

Then they'd snort and roll their eyes at the absurdity. She would laugh along because she didn't take herself too seriously.

Buoyed by the thought, Cassie made her way to the porch, took a deep breath and rang the doorbell.

"I don't think I'm cut out to do a show like this," said Logan McFadden. "I came home for Mom because she needs her family around her right now. I don't know if this show is a good idea, Sophie. It seems too chaotic, and that's the last thing she needs right now. Do you think we could convince her to bow out?"

His sister shot him an incredulous look across the small café table in her kitchen where they were having breakfast before the first production meeting of *Selling Sandcastle*, the reality show that would follow the ins and outs of their family's luxury real estate business.

"Do you think anyone wants to watch their life play out on national television?" Sophie shook her head. "We've already discussed withdrawing from the show, but this is what Mom wants. It's only for two months. We can do it for her."

Before her breast cancer diagnosis, their mother, Barbara "Bunny" Bradshaw McFadden, had been the driving force behind getting their family friend Dalton Hart to produce a show that followed Sandcastle Real Estate. Bunny had called in favors from her considerable contacts in the Junior League and the chamber of commerce. She'd hired the best photographers to showcase the family's agency and the town of Tinsley Cove in the best light, all to help Dalton realize his former hometown was a picture-perfect location for a reality show.

It had all paid off when everything had come together and Hart had agreed to do the show. Then, two weeks after receiving the impossibly good news, disaster struck in the form of Bunny's breast cancer diagnosis.

The sounds of the refrigerator and Sophie's kitschy Kit Cat clock, with its swinging tail and judging eyes that shifted from side to side with each tick, filled the otherwise silent kitchen.

Logan shook his head. "Two months can feel like a lifetime." Sophie gave him the stink eye. "But if it makes Mom happy, if this is what she wants, of course I'm in. That's why I came back. So she knows we're all here for her."

Sophie reached across the table and gave his hand a squeeze. "I know coming back here isn't easy for you, Loe, but she needs us right now. She needs all of us."

Logan stared into his coffee cup. He and Natalie had moved to California after they'd gotten married. They'd both been born and raised in Tinsley Cove, and they'd wanted to start their married life together in a new town, on their own terms.

They'd been in California for two years when she died. He'd forced himself to stick it out there because it seemed like it was all he had left of her, but now it was clear, no matter where he looked, he ran into reminders of what he'd had and what he'd lost.

Five years later, he'd learned that you couldn't take the people you loved for granted. If he'd figured that out sooner, Natalie might still be here.

He didn't have to like being back here. He didn't have to like this idiotic show that meant so much to his mom. If it made her happy…he'd do it.

"It's going to be all right," Sophie said. "I thought you might need a pep talk. That's why I invited you over for breakfast."

He'd come home after his mom had received the diagnosis and had stayed through her surgery. When the doctor said she was stable, he'd gone back to

California. With this health scare, Logan had never dreamed that she would continue to advocate for the reality show, but here they were a year later.

He'd put his life on hold and was back in Tinsley Cove for the two months and some change it would take to do this show.

He'd gotten into town late last night, in the middle of a hell of a storm. He was staying in one of the family's rental properties. His mom had wanted him to move into the family house, but Logan had been firm that he needed his own space.

It was an amiable compromise.

He and his sister had always been close. So, he wasn't surprised when she had invited him over for breakfast this morning.

She picked up the remnants of her bagel. "Think of this as the bagel of courage."

Logan snorted. "Okay. Why?"

"Hear me out," she said. "I think I'm on to something here. I can see the marketing campaign already."

"Yeah, well, the bagels of courage have to go on the back burner, because our lives are going to be consumed by a reality show."

"Yeah, well, eat your bagel of courage and you'll feel better," Sophie said as she glanced at the clock. "I need to finish getting ready. Do you want to drive to the meeting together?"

"Is that your not-so-subtle way of making sure I don't hightail it out of town?" he asked.

"Am I that obvious?" As she scooted back her chair and stood up, her cell phone rang.

She glanced at the screen.

"I need to take this call. It's Dave Anders, the AC guy, calling me back about when he can come by to look at the HVAC in the house next door. I left him a message last night because it seemed a little warm when the new tenant moved in. Just because we're going to be on television doesn't mean real life stops. It will be interesting juggling both."

"That's what I've been trying to say," Logan said.

She gave a little wave with one hand and answered her phone with the other. "Hey, Dave. Thanks for calling me back."

As Sophie's voice trailed off down the hall, Logan watched the crazy-eyed cat clock's bulbous eyeballs shift from side to side for a full minute before he swallowed the dregs of his coffee. He was pouring himself another cup when the doorbell rang.

Over the tick tock, tick tock, tick tock, his sister called, "Hey, Logan, I'm going to be on this call for a minute. Can you get the door?"

As the door opened, Cassie smiled her warmest smile and prepared to hold the edges of her dog food–bag dress, bob a curtsy and laugh with Sophie about the ridiculous morning, but Sophie wasn't the one standing in the doorway.

It was a guy.

Ohh…and a really cute guy at that.

She studied his face and guessed that he was somewhere around her age. Maybe a couple of years older. He had dark curly hair, dark eyes and a shadow of facial hair. It didn't look like he was growing scruff on purpose, but he didn't look unkempt, either. He looked…hot.

He wore jeans and a fitted white T-shirt that showcased broad shoulders and arms that looked like he didn't shy away from hard work.

He could've been in a Calvin Klein ad.

Apparently, the black truck in the driveway belonged to him and not the new friend that Cassie had imagined as she'd trekked across the side lawn.

Her hand fluttered to the neckline of her makeshift dress, and she pulled the heavy paper edges together. Taking a step backward on bare feet, she was aware that she was essentially naked except for her underwear and this large piece of heavyweight three-ply paper.

"Hi, I live next door." She hooked her thumb in the direction of her house. "Is Sophie at home?"

"She is, but she's busy."

"I'm so sorry to trouble you, but could I please use her phone?"

"Sophie doesn't have a landline. She's using her cell for a business call."

She waited for him to add, *Please feel free to come in and wait for her.* But he didn't.

She put her hand on the doorjamb. "Oh. Okay. Um…do you have any idea when she'll be free?"

"I have no idea. It sounded like she was going to be a while."

Cassie's heart pounded. "Well, okay… I… I—um… I locked myself out, and I need to get inside or I'm going to be late for something important. I don't know what to do—"

She choked on the words. All of a sudden, tears started falling to rival last night's storm. *Dammit.* She hadn't cried when she'd signed her divorce papers. She hadn't cried when she'd hugged Gabby goodbye. Now, as she stood here in front of this gorgeous stranger, wearing not her lucky dress but a ridiculous get-up made out of a dog-food bag, she couldn't stop the tears, and she hated herself for it.

"Hey, hey," the guy said, his tone markedly more sympathetic. "Don't cry."

He sighed and stepped back, away from her. He probably thought she was crazy. Or even worse. Dressed like this, with tears running down her cheeks, she probably looked like she'd surpassed crazy and face-planted at the intersection of unhinged and deranged.

"You can use my phone," he offered.

As he reached into his back pocket, she realized he hadn't been recoiling a moment ago but simply stepping out of the doorway, which had been filled with his considerable frame, to get his phone.

She sniffed. "Thank you. What a morning. Everything is going wrong. *Everything.*"

His face remained impassive. Clearly, he wasn't interested in hearing her sob story. So, she blinked away the tears and prepared to dial but stopped with her finger hovering over the phone screen.

"You wouldn't happen to have a phone book, would you? I need to call—" She was about to say, "The hotel where the production meeting is taking place" but stopped short as she remembered the confidentiality agreement. "I need to call *my office* because I'm going to be late, but I don't know the number off the top of my head. It's stored in my phone, which is in my house, and I'm locked out—"

She could hear the pitch of her voice rising with each word. She clamped her jaw shut, causing the tsunami of unspoken words to crest in the back of her throat and nearly choke her.

"A phone book?" He snorted. "Do they even make those things anymore?"

"Making fun of me is not helpful," she said. "I have no idea if they still make phone books, but I figured asking for one would be better than me swiping through your cell looking for your internet app and searching for the number myself."

His eyes widened, and he held up both hands in surrender.

"Okay. Point taken. You said you're locked out?"

She nodded.

"Sophie is on the phone, but I can ask her where she keeps the keys to the rental properties. How about if I just let you into your house? Wouldn't that be the easiest thing?"

Cassie gasped. "If you did that, you would be my hero."

For the briefest flit of a second, a smile quirked up the corner of his mouth and a dimple winked at her, but it was gone just as fast.

"What man would pass up the opportunity to be a hero?" he murmured, though he didn't sound very enthusiastic about the prospect. "Wait here. I'll be right back."

Before he turned, he reached out his left hand palm up.

"Oh, right. Your phone. Here you go."

As she handed it back to him, her gaze fell to his ring finger, which was bare. That probably meant he wasn't Sophie's husband. Yesterday when Sophie let her into the house, Cassie couldn't remember her mentioning that she was married—or even involved with anyone. Then again, they hadn't had much time to talk. Since this guy was in her house at this hour of the morning, answering her door, he was probably her boyfriend.

Hmm...lucky Sophie...even if this guy seemed proportionately as stoic as Sophie was warm and friendly. Cassie chalked it up to opposites attracting, but the laws of attraction were the least of her concerns right now. She needed to get to the Seaside Hotel for that meeting before they fired her...or worse yet, made her the show's diva villain.

Logan couldn't remember the last time a woman had called him a hero.

If ever.

He'd certainly been called plenty of other things in his life that weren't quite so flattering. After that compliment, how could he not help out the new tenant?

While he was back in town for the filming, he would dust off his real estate license and work as an agent for Sandcastle Real Estate. That was the so-called plan, even if it was just for show. He hadn't sold real estate since he'd left Tinsley Cove, opting instead to work as a general contractor, but he'd had the foresight to keep his license current.

Of course, he would pitch in where he was needed—like helping tenants who had locked themselves out.

As he and the neighbor strode silently toward her house, she walked about a step and a half ahead of him. Clearly, she was in a hurry.

That was a good thing, because as they walked,

he realized with every step she took, the very short dress-thing she was wearing rode up dangerously high in back, showcasing a pair of the longest, smoothest-looking tanned legs he'd seen in a long time.

He tried not to look, but he was a guy and she was attractive and those flawless legs were right in front of him.

He averted his gaze, trying to look away, but a flash of hot pink caught his eyes.

The polish on her toenails stood out in the green grass like tiny Easter eggs or neon jewels. Before he could stop himself, his eyes retraced the path up those long, tanned legs, and he caught himself wondering if they felt as smooth as they looked.

A frustrated growl sounded in the back of his throat.

"What was that?" She stopped and cast a glance over her shoulder, which made the dress ride up even higher.

Logan stopped, too.

As she smoothed the back of her dress with both hands, Logan looked everywhere but at her.

"Nothing." Logan bit off the word and spit it out.

She flinched, and he realized he might have sounded a little gruff. It was hard to tell over the strange buzzing in his head that had started when he opened the door and saw her standing there.

"Look, I'm sorry about this," she said. "I appreciate you coming to my rescue, but rest assured, I won't make a habit of locking myself out."

She turned around and started walking again.

This strange irritation needling him was weird.

It was idiotic to let a dress get to him. The woman was allowed to wear anything she wanted no matter how short or odd.

As he followed her across her driveway, he realized *irritated* probably wasn't the right way to describe how he felt...because what kind of a man would be irritated by a short dress, a nice pair of legs and pretty feet?

It was more like he was irritated at himself for noticing.

Surprised was a better word for it.

Thrown for a loop.

He'd been irritated because his coffee was getting cold. He was surprised at himself for being confounded by a woman he didn't even know.

She was attractive. Her blond hair fell to her shoulders in soft waves. She had green eyes that were similar in color to a piece of jade he used to have in the rock collection he'd prized when he was a boy.

He had no idea what had happened to all those rocks—to that piece of jade—or why her eyes made him think about it now.

He knew why the damned pink toenails bothered him. Because it seemed more intimate than hair and eye color. It bothered him because it had been a hell of a long time since he'd noticed anything like that about a woman who wasn't Natalie.

His heart constricted, and it hurt like hell.

That was also a surprise, because over the four-plus years since *that day*, he had existed in a world devoid of feeling and color.

He had lived with the loss every single second of every single day since the accident that had taken his wife. The pain had been so great that it had cauterized him into a state where he felt nothing, even if it hadn't stopped the loop of how things had gone down that day and the wish that he could go back and change the way that day had unfolded.

But it wasn't going to happen.

He would live with the consequences of his choices for the rest of his life. That's why he didn't deserve to notice a pair of nice legs and sexy pink toenails.

It didn't take a genius to know that returning to the place where he and Natalie had grown up together weeks before a significant anniversary of the accident that took her life would be triggering.

He would just have to get over himself. Shut off the emotion before it got the best of him. That's what he'd done in the past. He could do it now.

He shifted his attention to the ring of keys he'd been carrying at his side. As he walked, he sorted through the collection looking for the spare for 222 North Ridge Court, the address of his sister's new neighbor.

It had taken him a minute to find where Sophie kept the keys, but just as he'd suspected, the key-keeping system was exactly the same as it had been since his family had expanded their business to include rentals.

When he was a teenager, he would *borrow* the key to an unrented unit, and he and Natalie would sneak away. He blinked away the thought and refocused on finding the key he'd need to let the neighbor in. The sooner he could unlock the door, the sooner he could get back to his coffee…and away from her.

By the time they'd walked up onto the front porch, he had the key at the ready. A dog barked on the other side of the door as he unlocked it, but he didn't ask about the animal. She had the good grace not to try and engage him in conversation.

As he turned to leave, she had said, "Thank you. I appreciate your help."

He'd nodded. As she opened the door to step inside, the dog bolted out.

"Luna, stop!" she called.

Reflex had him lunging for the dog. As he caught it by the collar, which was a similar shade of hot pink as its owner's toenails, he realized the animal was a corgi. "Where do you think you're going, buddy?"

The dog didn't seem bothered by being captured. She good-naturedly jumped up onto his leg and licked his arm and his face. Despite himself, Logan smiled and scratched the dog's head with his free hand.

"Luna, get down!" the woman demanded. She started to bend down to take hold of the dog but then straightened up and tugged at the skirt. She tried a move that looked like an awkward curtsy but abandoned that, too.

She grimaced and glanced down at her dress.

"You've already been so nice and I hate to keep imposing," she said. "But would you mind wrangling her into the house? I would, but…"

For a split second, he was tempted to ask if she was always so much trouble. With her hot pink toes and tanned legs and little escapee dog, she was probably one of those high-maintenance women that swam in a sea of drama everywhere she went.

Instead, he swallowed the words and nodded.

Making a dig like that wouldn't be kind or helpful. Plus, she might think it was an invitation for conversation, which was the last thing he wanted.

She stepped away from the door and pressed her back against the porch wall, giving him ample room to maneuver the dog inside.

They managed to hand off the door, keeping it closed enough that Luna couldn't escape again but open enough so she could get inside.

"Thank you." She lingered with her hand on the doorknob. "I don't know what I would've done if I had to chase her all over the neighborhood. That's two saves in one day. I owe you one. Actually, I owe you two."

She smiled, and the way the morning light filtered onto the porch showed that the deep jade color in her eyes formed a ring around a kaleidoscope of gold, amber and moss green.

"No worries." He walked away.

At least she wasn't his neighbor. He wouldn't have to deal with her if she did make a habit of locking herself out. She would be Sophie's problem.

His sister was off the phone by the time he got back.

"Where'd you go?" she asked.

Logan held up the ring of keys. "Your new neighbor locked herself out."

"Cassie?" Sophie asked.

Logan shrugged. "Is that her name? I figured I'd let her in rather than bother you since you were busy."

"Thanks, Logan. That was nice of you. Cassie is so sweet. She just moved here from Florida."

That's probably where she got the tan…which wasn't his concern.

"I think she's single," Sophie singsonged.

"Good for her," Logan said. "I wish her all the best."

"Come on, don't you think she's pretty?"

"I didn't notice." He glanced at his watch. "We are going to be late if we don't get going, and I'm sure everyone will notice that."

Chapter Three

Traffic was mercifully light as Cassie made the fifteen-minute drive to the Seaside Hotel, giving her more than enough time to get there before the meeting.

Once she'd gotten back into the house, she'd dressed in the white Kate Spade pants and hot pink ruffled blouse. She'd put on her makeup and took Luna out to do her business with lightning speed. She'd started to put the little dog back in the house, but with the broken AC, it was just too hot inside.

Instead, she loaded Luna into the car and away they went to the meeting.

After all, it was just a meeting, and Luna was a good girl. Since the production company had rented the place, maybe they'd have more pull when it came to getting the AC fixed in a hurry.

"If not, you just might be on TV with me, Luna. What would you think about that?"

Cassie made a mental note to also ask them to have the automatic lock replaced with a standard one. She'd pay for it if they wanted her to. In the meantime, she should probably hide a key in the garage. She'd like to think she wouldn't lock herself out again, but she'd only be kidding herself.

Sophie's...*friend* hadn't seemed thrilled about helping her out. Cassie inhaled sharply, then bit her bottom lip. She hadn't even asked his name. She wanted to smack herself on the forehead.

She'd been in such a panic over being locked out and possibly being late, the only thing she could think about was getting back inside. Of course, the guy hadn't bothered to introduce himself, either, which was odd, given that he knew where to find the spare keys.

That was a little unsettling.

Oh, well. If he lived with Sophie, he was probably okay.

Maybe his terse manners were his way of establishing landlord-and-tenant boundaries, saying without saying that she shouldn't make a habit of asking for favors.

Even so, she should've asked his name. After all, he had saved her life—twice—so to speak.

The next time she ran into Sophie, she'd ask his name and find out his favorite kind of cookies and bake him a batch to show her appreciation.

At a stoplight she glanced at Luna, who was sitting in the back seat, strapped in by her harness, happily looking out the window. Cassie's gaze tracked to her own reflection in the rearview mirror. She grimaced. It wasn't her best makeup job, but it was all she'd had time for. At least they weren't filming today.

Even so, she could use a little more color. She was supposed to meet the rest of the cast and crew, and first impressions were everything.

She pulled out a tube of Charlotte Tilbury Amazing Grace lipstick from the makeup bag in her purse. She had just touched the color to her upper lip and had started to define the curve when the person behind her honked. She flinched and ended up drawing a red line from her lip into her right nostril.

"Ugh! Seriously?" Her heart hammered in her chest as she tried to wipe away the errant smear, but she only succeeded in smudging it more. Now, it looked like she had a lopsided ruddy mustache.

Cassie moaned. "Can this day get any worse?"

Luna barked.

"You're right, Luna," she said as she twisted the tube shut and replaced the cap. "There's no sense in tempting fate. Things will only get better."

The guy in the car behind her honked again, this time with more implied rage.

"Rude!"

She was tempted to give him the finger…but that wasn't her style.

Instead, she offered a quick wave to the angry driver and accelerated through the light.

"Luna, have you ever heard of the quote when you're having a bad day, that you should treat others better than the world was treating you?"

The little dog was quiet.

"Yeah, you're always sweet. I'm lucky you're mine. Everything will be fine, right?"

She whispered the words with the hope that she might believe it. So what if she hadn't been able to find her lucky dress? Then she'd locked herself out. Then Luna had almost escaped… Cassie started to change lanes, and she caught a glimpse of herself in the rearview mirror. Oh, yeah, and now she had a big red lipstick stain up her nose.

Dread washed over her. Had coming here been a bad idea? It had all been so rushed, and what made her think she had any business exposing herself on a reality show? It sounded like a recipe for humiliation.

All of a sudden she wanted to cry.

As if sensing her distress, Luna started to whimper.

"You know what, Luna? If you want to change your life, first you have to change your mind."

She was just full of platitudes this morning, wasn't she? Even so, she did need to reframe her thoughts.

She'd brought her makeup with her. She could fix the lipstick mishap once she parked in the hotel lot.

She'd find her lucky dress later. In fact, how lucky was she to have so many clothes to choose from?

She might have locked herself out, but Sophie's boyfriend had come to her rescue.

How lucky was Sophie to have such a gorgeous, capable, problem-solving boyfriend?

"How's this for changing the way I think? It's a good thing the guy who let me into the house is Sophie's boyfriend, because if Mr. Tall, Dark and Handsome wasn't involved with my landlord, I just might go way out on a limb and ask him out."

Of course, she could say that because he wasn't available.

"I'm just saying, if he was single, he would be my new type."

A flock of butterflies swarmed in her stomach.

"Don't you dare tell Sophie I said that, Luna. It's a secret between you and me."

Usually, she went for guys who were a little more talkative, but…the bottom line was it didn't matter. Surly hero guy was with Sophie, and Cassie would never betray her first friend in Tinsley Cove. Cassie knew what it was like to trust a friend with the man she loved and have them betray her so thoroughly it felt as if they'd ripped her heart out of her chest with their bare hands.

This new start was all about her.

"You know what, Luna? Scratch what I said about him not being available. *I* am emotionally unavailable. We have no room for a man in our lives, right? But woo-hoo, Sophie. Get it, girl!"

The little dog gave an agreeable *woof.*

Cassie laughed, willing herself to feel better as the GPS announced that she had arrived at her destination. She steered her car into the full parking lot of the Seaside Resort Hotel with fifteen minutes to spare.

She debated whether or not to valet park but decided against it when a family in a minivan vacated a space near her.

"How about that, Luna? We're early, and we just snagged a primo parking place. The day is already getting better."

After she parked, Cassie gazed up at the rambling, three-story resort that seemed to go on forever, spanning as far as her eyes could see. This place was different from the beachfront high-rises she was used to at home. This beautiful property resembled a majestic mansion, sprawling and proud. Its whitewashed exterior gave the impression that it would be better suited as the location of a romantic movie rather than a destination that hosted rowdy spring breakers like so many of the hotels in Florida.

"See, no need to be nervous," she reminded herself. "We just have to remember to breathe."

She checked her makeup and quickly repaired the lipstick damage. Fortified with fresh resolve, she stepped out of the car and retrieved Luna from the back seat, securing her leash. The fearless little dog trotted just ahead as if she were supposed to be here.

"I'm following your lead, Luna. Fake it until you make it."

Cassie checked her posture and walked toward the hotel's entrance.

She could hear the roar of the ocean. Seagulls squawked and circled overhead.

Something about the sounds soothed her nerves. *They were called laughing gulls.*

When she and her sister where little girls, they used to chase the gulls up and down the beach, imitating their cheerful *caw-caw-caws* and delighting at how the birds would scatter and fly away when rushed.

Caw-caw-caw. Caw-caw-caw. Caw-caw-caw.

They really did sound like they were laughing. She hadn't thought about that in years.

It was a good sign, Cassie told herself as she and Luna climbed the steps leading from the parking lot to the porte cochère.

The balmy, briny air smelled of sunshine and new beginnings. It was heavenly—restorative and healthy.

The breeze picked up her hair and playfully tossed it all around. Too bad today wasn't the day for wavy beach hair: There would be plenty of beach days ahead…but then again, who knew where the cameras would be, and who wanted to wear a bathing suit on national television?

As soon as she was under cover, she smoothed her hair back into place and hitched her purse onto her shoulder. People sat in rocking chairs lined up along the front of the hotel. Others chatted with the parking attendants and porters who manned rolling luggage racks piled high with suitcases that belonged to guests, some coming and others going.

A uniformed attendant smiled and opened the double doors as Cassie approached.

"Checking in?" he asked.

"No, I'm here for a meeting. Thanks, though."

"The concierge can direct you. You'll find the desk just inside to the right." He offered a quick salute in response to her thanks.

Relieved that he hadn't objected to Luna entering the building, Cassie paused in the hotel lobby, which was light and bright, decorated in shades of turquoise, sea-foam green and white. Potted palms and birds of paradise in huge planters sat atop the exquisite marble floor. The entire back wall of the lobby was made of glass and framed the ocean, showcasing it like a living painting.

A group of people dressed for business hurried

past her with purpose. A family clad in beachwear stood at the concierge desk, nodding as the hotel employee pointed to places on a map. It didn't look like they'd be wrapping things up anytime soon.

Cassie retrieved her phone from her purse and looked at the time. She still needed to find the meeting room. Rather than cutting it close waiting for the family to finish or interrupting them, she tapped her phone screen again and pulled up the email the production assistant had sent with information about where they were supposed to meet. As many times as she'd read the message, it was a wonder she hadn't memorized it.

She took the elevator up to the third floor and wound her way through a maze of green-carpeted hallways, following the directional signs until she found a set of wooden doors with a gold plaque that said Palm 322. She took a fortifying breath and simultaneously knocked and pushed open one of the doors wide enough to peer inside.

It was a typical conference room with a boardroom table and office chairs. What set it apart was the beautiful view of the Atlantic Ocean visible through the windows that ran along the east side of the room, similar to the hotel's lobby.

"Cassie, welcome—or would you prefer that I address you as Your Highness? *Huh? Huh?*" Dalton Hart, the producer she'd met at the audition, elbowed her and laughed at his own joke. "It's fabulous to see you again. Oh, and I see you brought a friend." He bent down and petted Luna on the head. "You truly must be royal if you travel with your corgi."

"Hi, Dalton. It's great to see you, too. This is Luna. The AC in the bungalow is acting up. I didn't want to leave her in a hot house."

"Of course," Dalton said. "I'll have one of my assistants mention that to the property management company. In the meantime, come in. Make yourself at home."

"Thank you. I can't believe I'm here. This is exciting."

She felt the weighty stares of the other people in the conference room, a group of four—a middle-aged man and woman and two guys who seemed around her own age. They all seemed to be sizing her up.

In addition to the four and Dalton, there were three more people in the room—two women and a guy seated at the table, who didn't even look up. Dalton bent down and was saying something to the guy, who was nodding as he focused on inputting something into a computer. Cassie hoped it was about fixing the AC. The women at the table seemed absorbed with sorting and stuffing papers into glossy folders.

"Hello, everyone, I'm Cassie." She directed the greeting to no one in particular and gave a little wave and her biggest smile, which felt a little too bright.

"Yes, this is Cassie Houston from Orlando, Florida," Dalton said. "Surprise! She will be part of the show, too."

When the group of four exchanged confused glances, Dalton added, "Get used to it, people. There will be many twists and turns as we travel down this road together. I'll explain how things will work as soon as everyone arrives. In the meantime, Cassie, meet some of your cast mates. This is Bert McFadden, founder and president of Sandcastle Real Estate, his lovely wife, Bunny, and their sons Forest and Owen McFadden, who also work for Sandcastle Real Estate. We're expecting two more McFadden siblings shortly."

Bert stepped forward and offered his hand. Cassie shook it, and they all exchanged polite greetings.

They were a handsome family. In fact, the two brothers were downright gorgeous—both were classically tall, dark and handsome. They seemed nice enough…after knowing them for, what, sixty seconds?

"Over here, I'd like to introduce everyone to my right-hand people, production assistants Seth, Kara and Zoe," Dalton said. "Yes, you heard that right. I have three right hands. I guess that's better than two left feet, right?"

Again, he laughed at his own corny joke as the PAs looked up from their work only long enough to offer quick greetings.

The McFaddens smiled and chuckled politely, as

if they were trying to be nice to the guy who had chosen them to be on television.

Dalton checked his watch. "We still have a few minutes before we're scheduled to begin. Please help yourself to some breakfast." He gestured to a sideboard set up with an array of fruit, yogurt, pastries, juices and hot beverages.

"Thanks for being early," Dalton said. "In this business, time is money, and I have a steadfast rule that to be early is to be on time, to be on time is to be late and to be late is to be *wonk, wonk, wonk*." He said the *wonk, wonk, wonk* part in descending sad notes and pulled an exaggerated unhappy face.

Cassie shuddered inwardly as she thought of the morning's close call. If not for Sophie's boyfriend, she might still be locked outside in her underwear.

She blinked away the thought and poured herself a cup of coffee. She'd just turned around to join the others when Sophie and hero guy walked into the conference room as if her thoughts had conjured them.

What in the world?

Did this show have a *Twilight Zone* theme? She certainly felt like she was caught in a strange alternate reality.

"I hope we're not late," Sophie said breathlessly. "If we are, it's all my fault. Even though we're doing the show, business is still going on and I was swamped this morning—"

With a *yip*, Luna took off across the room, her retractable leash expanding until she reached the guy who had rescued them earlier.

Sophie stopped midsentence as her gaze went from Luna, who was jumping up on the guy's leg, to Cassie.

She blinked and gave her head a little shake.

"Cassie? What are you doing here?"

Sophie watched hero guy stroke the corgi's head and then shot a confused look at the group, who must've been her parents and her brothers.

"Luna, off. Get down." The dog did as she was told and returned to Cassie's side.

Now, Sophie was looking at Dalton for answers.

"Cassie is my next-door neighbor. She just rented the house next door to me—" Sophie gasped and put her hands on her cheeks. "Oh my gosh. Cassie didn't rent the house. A corporation did. Cassie, are you part of the show? Dalton, did your production company rent the house the Cassie is living in?"

Dalton smiled broadly and nodded as if he'd just revealed the punch line of a joke.

"I had no idea," Sophie said. "Cassie, is that why you were so vague when I asked you what brought you to Tinsley Cove?"

Cassie nodded. "I was sworn to secrecy under penalty of death if I told anyone why I was here. Everything is happening so fast, when Dalton introduced your parents, I didn't put two and two together that your last name was also McFadden."

"I know," Sophie said. "We were sworn to secrecy, too. I had no idea that the corporation that rented the bungalow had anything to do with the show."

"That's exactly why you weren't supposed to talk about the show before now," Dalton said. "We like that element of surprise."

Sophie pointed at Dalton. "Ah, I see what you did there."

"That was your first test, and you all passed with flying colors." Dalton did a slow clap. "Good job, Team *Sandcastle*. In case you were wondering, *Selling Sandcastle* is the name of your show. Because mansions on the beach—and the company is Sandcastle Real Estate. Get it? *Huh? Huh?*"

The others made approving sounds, but Cassie was stuck on what Dalton had said earlier—that two more McFadden *siblings* would arrive. That meant that Mr. Tall, Dark and Handsome wasn't Sophie's boyfriend. He was her brother.

The butterflies startled and swarmed in her stomach again. She tried to ignore the thrill that spiraled through her, as if she'd just been given a gift.

Now that she saw the two side by side, there was an uncanny resemblance.

Luckily, Bert provided some distraction. "To be honest, it did cross my mind that the show might be renting the house, but since it was all so hush-hush,

I wasn't going to ask. Sophie does a good job with the application checks. To be honest, we do a lot of short-term leases for companies that want to bring their staff on retreats and or offer beach vacations as incentives. As long as the application checks out and the security deposit is paid, we don't need a sworn statement about who they are or how they'll use the places."

Dalton smiled his Hollywood smile. "As I said, before, get used to it, folks. *Selling Sandcastle* will be full of surprises.

"Speaking of surprises," he said. "Sophie, I know you and Cassie have already met. And I just found out that Logan and Cassie have met, too. Earlier this morning? *Huh? Huh?*"

Wait. What?

Dalton waggled his brows as if he'd caught them in a tryst.

When neither of them answered, Dalton said, "Come on, you two, you know exactly what I'm talking about. Spill the tea."

How did Dalton know this? Was Logan—that was his name, right? Logan? Was he in on this? Had he set her up? Her mind raced as she tried to put the pieces of the puzzle together. Even though she couldn't figure it out, clearly he wasn't the Good Samaritan she'd given him credit for.

Cassie's face went hot, and she glared at Logan.

Mister you can forget about those cookies I was going to bake for you.

"It really wasn't a big deal," Sophie said to Dalton.

Logan shook his head. "She locked herself out of the house, and I let her in. But how did you find out?"

All eyes were on Dalton. "The footage came through on the doorbell camera. When we leased the place, we got access to the doorbell intercom, which also has a camera. It went off this morning, and I saw Cassie and Logan were on the front porch. Here, take a look."

Cassie froze as Dalton picked up a remote control off the table and pressed some buttons. Blackout shades slid down, covering the room's windows, and a projection screen appeared on the wall at the head of the conference table.

This can't be happening.

But, oh, yes, it was.

Cassie's heart hammered in her chest as her image appeared on screen, larger than life, in that hideous dog food–bag dress. The footage showed her and Logan standing on the front porch of her bungalow as he unlocked the door and then caught Luna before she could escape.

What was worse than being caught on camera in the dog-food bag was the camera was at just the right angle to catch Cassie staring at Logan like she was starving and he was a biscuit dripping with butter.

Sure, he was good-looking…from all angles, but she hadn't realized she'd looked so…desperate.

Well, that was because she hadn't known she was being recorded.

From here on out, she would be on her guard.

Total poker face 24-7, which would be totally annoying…but better on guard than embarrassed like this.

"This is all very sweet." Dalton laughed. "I do believe I detect some chemistry between the two of you? *Huh? Huh?* I can't be the only one who sees it."

Dalton glanced around as if he expected a chorus of affirmation, but all he got were virtual crickets.

He changed tactics. "I'm sorry, I have to ask. What the hell are you wearing in the video, Cassie? Is that some kind of avant-garde dressing gown?"

Cassie was so mortified that she couldn't answer.

She scanned the faces of her new cast mates—except for Logan. She couldn't even look at him. The McFaddens looked baffled, staring at the bizarre black-and-white footage looping on the screen, as if they weren't quite sure what they were looking at.

All Cassie could think was, *wonderful. Just wonderful.*

She'd watched enough reality television to understand embarrassing things were bound to happen while she was on the show, but she hadn't realized she'd be on the hot seat so soon.

Finally, she shrugged. "Maybe you'd better re-think that allowance for a wardrobe stylist?"

Before Dalton could respond, Logan said, "Are you spying on us? Because I don't remember giving permission for hidden cameras. I mean, is this even legal?"

"I told you this was footage from the doorbell cam." Dalton's smile remained, but his voice had a slight edge.

"I heard you," Logan said. "But can you please clarify if there will be hidden cameras involved in this project, because that would be a deal breaker for me. I didn't sign up for one of those frat house reality shows."

"Logan," Bert admonished.

"What?" Logan snapped. "Having our lives filmed for television is intrusive enough, but hidden cameras cross the line. That's a total invasion of privacy."

Cassie agreed. Hidden cameras would be creepy.

"Dalton, I'm sorry," Bunny said. "Let's just chalk this up to first-day jitters."

Logan frowned. He opened his mouth to say something but must've thought better of it, because he clamped his jaw shut.

"No apologies needed," Dalton said. "It's fine. It's all fine."

He stared at Logan for a few beats before saying, "Actually, this is quite excellent. For a show like this to make a splash, we need conflict. It's great that you don't want to be here, Logan. In fact, I'm going to amend the preliminary production schedule to include scenes that reflect this angst."

Dalton's smile and blunt tone posed an eerie juxtaposition.

If Logan didn't want to be here, why was he here? That seemed to be the million-dollar question.

Dalton clasped his hands in front of him. "Now that we've gotten that out of the way, why don't we all gather around and get this show on the road? Have a seat, everyone. My assistant Kara has prepared packets of information that you'll find interesting and helpful. Everyone be sure and grab one. We will email each of you tomorrow's call sheet. Before you leave, double-check the email address we have for you. It's on the paper Zoe is passing around."

As everyone gathered around the table, the fact that Dalton hadn't denied the use of hidden cameras during the course of the show niggled at Cassie. She thought about asking but held off so that Dalton could kick off the meeting. Maybe he would talk about it later.

Dalton broke into his spiel about how he'd gone to high school with Forest McFadden and had known the family most of his life.

"I would like to welcome the cast of *Selling Sandcastle*. When Bert and Bunny contacted me with the idea of Top Drawer Productions doing a reality show that chronicles the day-to-day action in a luxury real estate firm, I knew we were on to something. I put together a proposal and took it to the Home, Hearth and Garden Network, worked my magic, and here we are. We have the green light to do a five-episode first season. It's scheduled to air this fall."

Maybe Logan would bring up the hidden cameras, since he'd seemed so opposed to them. Cassie glanced at him and was surprised to see him staring at her. He had leaned back in his chair with his arms crossed over his chest. His brows were knit into a scowl, and his full lips were pursed together so tightly the first thought that popped into her mind was, *be careful or your face will stick that way.*

The absurd thought made her want to giggle.

Before she could stop it, a smile broke through and she had to bite her lip to keep from laughing out loud.

Why did she always have the urge to laugh at inappropriate moments? Before she could even start the list of sad and somber thoughts that would rein in her runaway emotions—a hint of a grin tugged up the corner of Logan's mouth.

It wasn't exactly a warm smile, but at least it wasn't the soul-piercing frown he'd directed her way before.

And there was that impossibly attractive dimple.

Her mind flashed back to the comment Dalton had made about sensing chemistry between them.

Oh, no. Did Logan think she was flirting with him? Please, let that not be the case.

She felt a rush of prickly heat creep up her neck and spread across her cheeks.

If he hadn't thought it then, he probably did now.

"And when Cassie and Logan are finished flirting with each other," said Dalton, pointedly looking at them, "we can discuss their respective roles on the show and the filming schedule."

Chapter Four

Logan wasn't going to dignify Dalton's sophomoric flirting dig with a response, but Cassie had taken the bait.

"We're not flirting," she protested as swaths of pink bloomed on her cheeks.

Logan tried to catch her eye, to telegraph that she shouldn't give him the satisfaction. By responding she was only adding fuel to the fire.

"Well, well, well, what do you know?" Dalton rubbed his hands together. "The lady doth protest too much, methinks." He looked back and forth between Cassie and Logan. "*Huh? Huh?* I think we're on to something here."

No one in the room said a word.

"It works," Dalton said. "Think about it. You're both single. The two of you look good together. I like it. I want you two to keep it up."

Logan stared down at his hands, which were steepled on the table. It felt like the only safe place to look. He fought the urge to get up and walk out.

If he'd known there were hidden cameras and there'd be attempts to pair him up romantically, he never would've agreed to this. Even if it was all fake for television.

But then he glanced at his mother and felt like a jerk.

Since her cancer diagnosis, she had taken great pride in eliminating fear and reticence from her life. She had adopted a *you only live once* attitude, and she was bound and determined that every person she loved would learn to live in such a carefree fashion.

She was the one who had signed them up to do this show as a family. In a moment of weakness, Logan had said that on the long-shot chance that the network green-lighted the show, he would come back to Tinsley Cove and be part of it. The minute his mother had heard that there was a chance that all four of her grown children would all be together again, she was on a mission. Of course, it would be good for Sandcastle Real Estate's business.

She had a long list of reasons they had to do the show.

Even so, Logan had been stunned when he'd heard

the network had given the nod. He'd quickly come up with his own list of why he wouldn't be able to participate, but in the end he agreed to take part, because if he had learned one thing since Natalie died, it was if something was *that* important to someone you loved, sometimes you just had to suck it up and do it for them.

Fate could be a bitch. She didn't always give second chances.

Dalton nodded with a self-satisfied smile as he scribbled some notes on a pad of paper.

"Yeah, this is good stuff, people," he murmured.

Then he dropped his pen on the table and clapped his hands together once. "Okay, why don't we start by having each of you introduce yourselves? I know the McFaddens already know each other, but this will give me a chance to catch up with what you've been doing with yourself over the years, and of course, it will give your cast mate Cassie the opportunity to get to know you better. Forest, why don't you start us off?"

"I'm single," Forest said. "I've worked as a broker for Sandcastle Real Estate since graduating from the University of North Carolina at Chapel Hill and returning to Tinsley Cove. Now I'm running for mayor."

Dalton smiled. "Yes, the mayor bit will bring an interesting dynamic. It will be fun to follow you as you campaign."

"Something to consider is the Picnic in the Park event downtown," Forest said. "It's happening soon. I'm sponsoring a booth, and we're giving away free hot dogs and snow cones as well as campaign buttons and yard signs. If you haven't already signed up to help me serve the food—" Forest smiled pointedly at Cassie and lifted his brows. "We still need help covering the last shift. We could use your help, but I know it's a weekend, and no pressure if you already have plans."

Cassie raised her hand. "I don't mind helping for an hour or so."

"We will put that on the filming schedule," Dalton said. "Zoe, did you get that?"

Owen, Bert and Bunny followed, mostly talking about their roles in the family business.

Bunny didn't mention the cancer battle and her recovery.

Finally, it was Cassie's turn. "I'm Cassie Houston. I was born and raised in Orlando, Florida. I'm…" She trailed off, and Logan saw her throat work. "I'm divorced, and my background is in interior decorating. So to speak. If Sandcastle Real Estate has any homes that need to be staged, I'm your go-to gal."

A nervous laugh escaped.

Dalton's eyes widened and he held up a finger. "You've just given me an excellent idea. Bert, if I'm hearing this right, only McFaddens work for Sandcastle Real Estate. It's a family-owned and-operated business. You've never had any nonfamily employees, right?"

"Right," Bert said. "That's not necessarily by design. It's just the way we've grown the business."

"For the sake of the show," Dalton said, "that's going to change. Hear me out. Bert, you are going to hire Cassie as an in-house staging expert. She will be the first non-McFadden to come on board. Since Logan was away, he wouldn't have been here for the hiring process, and he won't have say in the new hire. I could imagine that Logan might take issue with that. He'd feel out of favor since he was cut out of the process. See where I'm going with this?"

The room was silent.

"That doesn't make sense," Logan asked. "Why would I take issue with that?"

"Because we need drama," Dalton said. "Drama is key here. It's what makes people tune in. Understand?"

"Not really," Logan said.

"You have to understand. Because we all need to be on the same page. Think about it, Logan. You've been away and after the prodigal son returns, you learn that Dad has hired the first nonfamily employee and he's cut you out of the decision. See where I'm going?"

"But I'm not really the *prodigal* son in the true sense of the parable. A prodigal is a person who leaves home and acts irresponsibly, but when they get home they're repentant. I wasn't irresponsible."

A lump formed in Logan's throat because he *had* been irresponsible—if he'd been the good husband, the bigger person, Natalie might be alive right now.

"Okay, but most people hear 'prodigal son' and they think *son who went away and came home*, period." Dalton said. "Let's not split hairs. We don't have to overcomplicate it. So, Bert, after Logan takes issue with you hiring Cassie, you're concerned that you upset Logan. So, you make it up to him by asking him to supervise Cassie. That's what will throw them together."

"If I've been away for several years, why would I show Cassie the ropes? Seems like I'll need someone to show *me* around."

Dalton didn't respond. "So, we have Logan's resentment over the new hire that's tempered by his simmering chemistry with Cassie. It's going to be great."

Everyone was quiet. Until Cassie asked, "So, do I get a say in this?"

"No." Dalton flashed a smile at her.

She flinched and opened her mouth as if she was about to say something but stopped and frowned.

"So, wait a minute," Bert said. "How is this going to work? Do I have to pay Cassie a salary?"

Dalton pursed his lips together and shrugged as if he was thinking about the answer.

Finally, he said, "Well, Cassie is an interior designer. I hope you don't expect her to donate her services."

"Actually, I'm a decorator. Interior designers have degrees in interior design."

Dalton held up a silencing hand. "She is going to help you make the most out of your listings. Because, as we've already established, Sandcastle Real Estate's business isn't going to stop while we're filming. The expertise she brings will help you sell the houses faster and for more money than if they weren't staged like model homes. She's worth it. Plus, if staging services are something Sandcastle Real Estate can offer clients who are selling their houses, and other agencies don't offer that, it will set your office apart from the others. It's a win-win for everyone. Especially you as the broker."

Bert gave a one-shoulder shrug and lifted his brows as if the idea was growing on him. He glanced at Bunny, who nodded enthusiastically.

"Do you want the job?" he asked Cassie.

She smiled. "I guess I do."

"Okay, you're hired. On Dalton's recommendation. What if we give you a cut of the commission on each property that you stage that sells?"

"Sounds fair to me," she said.

"If you can come into the office tomorrow, we can talk specifics. We've scheduled a photographer to take photos of an important listing on Thursday.

It would be great if we could get some furniture in there before the shoot. I know some North Carolina furniture manufacturers that may be able to help us out. I'll get their information together for you."

"That's the spirit," Dalton said. "That's how we're going to capture the day-to-day magic that happens at Sandcastle Real Estate." Dalton held up his hands, curving his fingers into a frame as if he were capturing a vision. "We need to show the family dynamics as well as the gorgeous beachfront mansions that you sell. That's what will set the show *Selling Sandcastle* apart from all the other real estate shows."

Dalton snapped his fingers twice. "Zoe, take a note. First call will be tomorrow morning at 8:00 a.m. sharp. We'll start with the Logan and Bert new-hire confrontation at the Sandcastle Real Estate office. Then Cassie can come in to 'meet' with Bert." Dalton drew air quotes around the word *meet*. "We can stage it like Cassie and Logan are being introduced for the first time.

"Logan, I know you'll need a chance to digest everything, but trust me, the drama about cutting you out of the hiring decision will work. Come in with the attitude that you're going to outsell your brothers. In fact, your goal is that you're determined to be the top seller. That's good. *Huh? Huh?*"

Dalton smiled and looked around the room at each person as if he'd just come up with the answer to world peace. The others greeted his genius with more crickets.

Just when the silence was getting awkward, Bunny said, "Cassie, tell us more about yourself, dear. Is your family in Orlando?"

Everyone's attention shifted to Cassie. She glanced down at her hands, which were folded in front of her on the table. "Both of my parents are gone. It's just my sister, Gabriella, and me. Gabby is still in Orlando."

"I'm so sorry for your loss," Bunny said. "That's difficult, but it's good that you and your sister have each other."

Cassie nodded but fell uncharacteristically silent. Logan understood. Talking about loss was hard.

"Logan you're up next, dude," said Dalton. "Tell us what you've been doing for the past decade. And I know Cassie will be happy to learn a little more about you."

Logan's gaze flicked over to her, and he caught her shifting in her seat. It appeared that she didn't like this pressure any better than he did.

"I'm a widower." He figured he might as well lead with it. "I lost my wife almost five years ago. She and I lived in California, but now I'm back in Tinsley Cove."

His gaze flicked to his mother. He realized he didn't know how much she'd told the producers about her illness. She'd wanted this show so badly and had voiced fears that if they learned she had been sick, they might not go forward with the show. So, he left it at that.

"I was sorry to hear about Natalie's accident," Dalton said in an uncharacteristic moment of realness. "I hadn't seen her since high school. I'm sorry for your loss."

Logan answered with a single nod and hoped that was the end of the conversation that involved Natalie.

"What have you been doing with yourself over the past four-plus years?"

"I've been working in construction," he said.

"Logan, you're too modest," said Bunny. "He was a contractor. He had his own company."

He certainly didn't want to go there.

"*Had?*" Dalton asked. "What happened to it?"

"Now that I'm back in Tinsley Cove, I'll be joining the family business," he said. "I have a real estate license. I'll be selling houses...at least while I'm here. Isn't that what this show is about?"

"You didn't answer my question," Dalton said. "Tell me about your company in California."

"What about it?"

"Is someone holding down the fort while you're gone?"

He should've been prepared for this. It was bound to come up. The only way to handle it was to be direct. To hit it straight on.

"I closed up shop about a year after my wife died.

You know what? This is a good time to establish some boundaries. I'm cool with you following me on a day-by-day basis, but my life in California, my past has nothing to do with this show. Do we understand each other?"

Dalton didn't answer him. Instead, he asked, "Is Natalie's family still in town?"

"Why?" Logan asked. "Did you hear what I said a minute ago? If you're thinking of incorporating them into the show, it's a hard no from me."

"Keep an open mind," Dalton said.

Logan slammed his hand down on the table. "You're obviously not hearing me, Dalton."

"You guys, please." Bunny held out her hands as if separating a pair of fighters. "Dalton, please try to see this from Logan's point of view. It's difficult to lose someone you love. If you haven't been through it yourself—and I hope you haven't—it may be hard to fully understand. Not a day goes by that we all don't miss our Natalie. She was such a sweet girl and an important part of our family. So, if Logan seems a bit hesitant about this idea of delving into his past or pairing him up with Cassie, that's why. No offense to you, dear." Bunny turned to Cassie. "I'm sure you're a sweetheart, too, but Logan is still grieving. He's not trying to be difficult."

"Bunny," Bert said, "Logan is a grown man. He can speak for himself."

"Yes, thanks, I can. So, let's just—"

Logan made a slashing motion through the air.

"You're here now, and that's the most important thing," Bunny said.

Dalton blew out an audible breath. "Yeah, but it's been almost five years. You're young, dude. You can't spend the rest of your life in limbo...or worse."

Logan balled his hands into fists. If he stayed in this room, he was going to explode. He couldn't bring himself to look at Cassie, so his gaze landed on his mother, who was looking at him with such pity, that was all it took to propel him to his feet.

He could deal with a lot, but this was too much.

"Look, I'm not going to do this. Not right now," he said. "Excuse me. I need to get out of here for a minute."

Chapter Five

After the conference room door closed behind Logan, Dalton continued as if nothing had happened.

"Don't forget to check your email, boys and girls," he said. "Zoe will send each of you a call sheet as soon as everything is ironed out. However, I can tell you that we will kick things off tomorrow morning with Bert and Logan in the Sandcastle office. After that we will move over to your listing on Figure Eight Island. The property owners have given us permission to shoot tomorrow. Cassie, this scene will be with you and Logan. We have a very tight shooting schedule. I'm counting on one of you to give Logan the heads-up. With that, it's a wrap for today."

Dalton and his crew cleared out of the conference

room first, saying that they needed to scout a couple of locations to have in their back pockets for future scenes. Bert, Bunny, Forest and Owen stayed just long enough to exchange general pleasantries and assure Cassie that they were looking forward to getting to know her better, but each had appointments.

As the sons left the room, Bert handed Cassie a card. "Call my assistant and set up an appointment so that we can talk privately about this staging job."

Bunny put a hand on his arm. "Honey, Dalton said he wanted to record the exchange."

Bert grimaced. "Yeah, well, I'd like for Cassie and me to be on the same page before we commit everything to film."

"Talking about particulars before we're on camera sounds like a good idea, but I'm flexible," said Cassie as she shifted Luna's leash from one hand to the other. The little dog got up from where she'd been sleeping under Cassie's chair and stretched. "I'll call your office later this afternoon and see what we can set up."

After they left, the conference room seemed eerily quiet, and at least a dozen questions flooded Cassie's brain. What were they going to do with the footage of her in the dog food–bag dress? And Dalton had managed to get away without answering the hidden-camera question.

In the meantime, she'd just have to be careful.

As she was gathering her things, she noticed that

Logan had left the conference room so fast he'd forgotten his folio and the packet of production information on the table. She could walk it next door and give it to his sister.

Or maybe she should just leave it here. He'd probably come back for it.

When she stepped into the hallway, she saw Sophie and Logan a few feet away deep in discussion. Before Cassie could lock the leash, Luna bolted toward Logan and jumped up on his leg.

"Hello," Logan said to the little dog as he scratched her ears.

"Luna, off!" Cassie said. "I'm so sorry. She really does have better manners than that. She just seems to lose her head every time she's around you, Logan."

Oh, no. Had she seriously just said that out loud?

In her head, it hadn't sounded quite so autobiographical.

No, wait! Autobiographical wasn't the right word…it wasn't how she, *herself*, felt about Logan. Even if she did become a bundle of nerves when she was around him. That's just because after everything Dalton had said about chemistry and how good they would look on camera together, she just wanted to cringe.

Maybe he hadn't noticed. The stormy scowl he'd worn a moment ago had softened into an almost smile as he looked at the animal.

"Aww, hello, Luna," Sophie said. "And Cassie, I

am still trying to wrap my mind around the fact that you're going to be on the show, too. I had no idea. But you know what? It's great. It's going to be so much fun. Right, Logan?"

"Sure it is." His face darkened again. He straightened and crossed his arms over his chest.

"Yeah, about that… Can we talk for a minute?" Cassie asked.

When he didn't answer right away, she said, "If now isn't a good time, we could do it later. I just wanted to clear the air about a couple of things."

"This sounds interesting." Sophie glanced at her watch. "But as much as I'd love to stay while you two are getting acquainted, I need to run. The air-conditioning repairman is meeting me at your place in fifteen minutes to take a look at the HVAC unit. Was it any better this morning?"

Cassie shook her head and explained how she had cranked the thermostat down, but it hadn't done any good.

"I'm so sorry," Sophie said. "When I did the walk-through the day before you arrived, it seemed fine. I guess you never know when those things are going to break down. Do you mind if we go inside while you're not there?"

"Have at it," Cassie said.

Sophie touched Cassie's arm. "Never fear. I'll get it taken care of. If he can't fix it straight away, I'll send Logan over with a window unit for you to use until it's working again. Logan can install it for you since he's handy."

Sophie smiled a knowing smile that Cassie tried to ignore.

Once Sophie had disappeared around the corner, Cassie said, "Thank you."

"For what?" Logan asked.

"Actually, I owe you a couple of thank-yous," she said.

"I'm sure it's all good," he said.

"First, thank you for coming to my rescue this morning after I locked myself out. I haven't gotten used to the self-locking door. Why would anyone ever put a self-locking thingamabob on a door? It's just asking for trouble."

"Didn't Sophie warn you about it?"

"I haven't even had time to unpack, much less get used to an autolocking door," she said. "That's why I'd locked myself out. Well, actually, I didn't lock myself *out* out. I mean, I was in the garage. I went out there to look for a box with the dress I was going to wear to work today—" She glanced down at her clothing. "Obviously not this outfit— or what I was wearing when you helped me. Long story short, my dress wasn't there and all I had was that dog-food bag, and thank goodness I had it because—" She shuddered. "I don't think the neighborhood would've appreciate me walking around in my birthday suit."

* * *

He did not need to know that.

Or at least he tried to tell himself that as the image of Cassie naked sprang unbidden into his head. He held up his hand.

"You don't have to explain."

She inhaled sharply. "Wait, just to be clear, I wasn't literally walking around in my birthday suit. I was in my underwear. So, don't be picturing me naked."

He tried to blink away the image, but it had already burned into the retina of his mind's eye. The hallway suddenly felt about ten degrees warmer, and he was at a loss for words.

Rarely was he ever stunned speechless. He always had plenty to say, even if he chose not to verbalize his thoughts. Unlike Cassie, who seemed to say everything that popped into her head.

"I felt like I needed to explain why I was dressed like that—"

He held up his hand and opened his mouth to assure her that she didn't need to say any more. She touched his forearm and gave it a little squeeze, which sent a strange *zing* spiraling through his body as she kept talking.

She didn't use full stops in her sentences. Instead, she used place holders via drawn-out words, commas and conjunctions. He'd never been particularly good at English, so he had no idea why he was mentally diagramming her sentences.

Probably because it distracted him from the peculiar way her touch had made him feel and the way it seemed to ripple through him when he saw himself unwrapping that dog-food bag to see what was—or wasn't—underneath.

Good God, enough. He wasn't fifteen years old.

He grimaced and pressed his hand to his eyes, trying to knock out the image.

"Are you okay?" She was touching his arm again.

He cleared his throat and stepped back, allowing some extra space between them. "I'm fine."

She closed the distance.

"As I was saying, I feel like such an idiot, and the fact that you didn't embarrass me during the meeting when Dalton made such a big deal out of the doorbell-camera footage proves that you are a real gentleman."

A gentleman? He'd been called a hero and a gentleman in one day.

"In fact, Logan, it almost seemed as if you steered him away by pressing the issue of hidden cameras, which we never fully got to the bottom of—"

"What would I gain by embarrassing you?" Logan asked.

Cassie blinked. "Well… I don't know. A lot of people would've jumped at the opportunity to make a joke at someone else's expense. Not everyone would've been as nice as you were."

He frowned. "If that's how the people you know treat you, you need new friends," Logan said.

"Oh, if you only knew. That's precisely why I'm here in Tinsley Cove, but that's a story for another day. Thank you for your discretion, Logan. I owe you one. So just know, I will always have your back while we're filming this show."

"Thank you for that," he said. "I appreciate it."

A mischievous smile spread over Cassie's pretty face. "Since I have your back, you have to have mine. No filing away the lockout to use as drama fodder later on."

"I hadn't thought about that, but thanks for the idea."

She narrowed her eyes at him. "For the record, a gentleman doesn't extort a lady. Oh, that was a joke, wasn't it? Never mind. Forget I said that, okay?"

For the first time since they'd started this conversation, silence stretched between them.

It lasted maybe ten beats.

"Is that all?" he asked. "I'm not used to this much silence when I'm around you."

He smiled to let her know he was joking.

She sighed and bit down on her bottom lip.

"I always talk too much when I'm nervous," she said.

"Don't be nervous. We're all in this together, and you and I have already declared our alliance."

She shrugged again and sighed, a world of vulnerability swimming in her green eyes, and Logan suddenly felt protective of her.

"It's just that everything is so new, and it's all happening so fast. I've lived in Florida my whole life. My sister is there. She and I are so close. But I'm also leaving behind a lot of bad memories. I keep going back and forth between being homesick and happy to make a fresh start. But now Dalton is pushing us together and you know how he keeps talking about chemistry between us. It's—"

She covered her mouth with her hand.

"There I go again," she said through her fingers. "I'm sorry. It's just that… I'm thinking…"

Who had done such a number on her that she needed a fresh start? She'd mentioned an ex-husband…but that was none of his business, even if they both seemed to be on a quest to start over.

Do not let this woman draw you in.

Nothing was going to happen between them— even if it was scripted for TV. His ability to love and trust had died along with Natalie.

Not that love and trust had a thing to do with the supposed chemistry that was to lead to a made-for-television romance to keep fans tuning in.

All of Tinsley Cove would be watching. Despite everything that had happened before Natalie died, it would be disrespectful to her and her family to chase after another woman.

Maybe they should come up with a plan to give Dalton the on-screen drama he needed for the show but that would also allow them to keep their dignity.

"I just thinking maybe we should…"

When she didn't finish her sentence, Logan asked, "What are you thinking?"

"This." She leaned in and pressed her lips to his.

For the span of a heartbeat, Logan was disoriented, as if the axis of his world had tipped and left him hanging upside down.

A voice in his head said, *Stop. You shouldn't be doing this.* But his body was singing another tune. As Cassie opened her mouth to deepen the kiss, his nerve endings sizzled like live wires, making his body vibrate until he couldn't hear anything over the need rushing through his veins.

He pulled her tighter and leaned into the kiss as if his next breath depended on it.

The next thing he knew, she'd pulled back slightly. Still holding on to him, she stared up at him dreamily.

"I was thinking we should get that out of the way so we can move on with what we need to do," she said. "It wasn't so bad, was it?"

After the kiss, after Cassie had stammered, "It wasn't so bad, was it?" Logan had just stood there looking at her in stunned silence.

She stood there for about three seconds taking in the look on his face, and then she turned around and walked Luna straight to the elevator.

Logan didn't call out after her or try and stop her.

As the elevator doors slid shut, she was alone with her dog, and she groaned, "Ugh. Ugh ugh ugh," and softly knocked her forehead against the brassy doors.

Luna let out a little bark.

"I know, that was dumb."

On what planet was spontaneously kissing a man like Logan a good idea? She'd known him for less than a day, and he was clearly still toting around tons of baggage over his late wife, who had probably been perfect and had probably never put him on the spot like Cassie had just done.

"'Hello, my name is Logan. I'm a widower. I'm not interested in pretending to have chemistry with you.' So, what do I do, Luna? I kiss him."

Luna sat down and pressed her body against Cassie's leg. The weight of her was comforting.

"You know the worst part, Luny? The worst part was I think Dalton is right about the chemistry. That kiss was kind of explosive."

Cassie pressed her hand to her lips. They still tingled with the feel of him.

"He kissed me back."

She bit down on her bottom lip, trying to make the sensation of him go away. But it didn't.

The doors opened onto the hotel lobby. Instead

of going out to her car, where she could continue to cringe and berate herself in private, she turned the other way and walked Luna down to the beach.

As Cassie slid off her sandals, the little dog turned her nose up to the wind, did a few doughnut runs in the sand and then scampered after a colony of gulls flocked together at the water's edge. They scattered and flew off, their squawks still sounding like laughter.

That, coupled with the roar of the waves and the constant whoosh of the wind, drowned out the chastising voices in her head and reminded her that she shouldn't take herself so seriously.

After walking a short distance down the beach, she sat down in the sugary sand so Luna could rest. The little dog plopped down beside her.

"It is what it is."

It was just a kiss that didn't mean anything.

Actors kissed each other all the time and stayed professional. Good grief, actors did love scenes and kept it together.

Of course, that immediately inspired thoughts of getting naked with Logan, and she realized she was either going to be a total wreck around this man or she was going to have to get over herself.

It would help if she could stop thinking about him. He was like a song that had earwormed itself into her brain. The best way to get something like that out of her head was to hear the whole song. Sing it from start to finish. Wallow in it. Become saturated by it.

Then it will leave you alone.

Would it work with Logan? It was worth a try.

She tipped her face up to the warm sun, closed her eyes and let her imagination run wild.

In her mind, she and Logan stood facing each other on the beach. She took his face in both of her hands, reveling in his strong jawline and the sheer beauty of his features.

She ran her hands through his dark, wavy hair. Her hands drifted down, over his broad shoulders, then farther down over his strong arms and around back, cupping that perfect butt.

Mmm... Logan had her favorite body type—big and sturdy, making her feel soft and feminine next to him...or underneath him...

The thought made her draw in a sharp breath. The heady scent of the briny ocean air melded with the awareness that spiraled through her body. She shifted back onto her elbows and relived the kiss they'd shared, only this time Logan was the one who initiated it... Putting his arms around her, pulling her close. His lips moving slowly over hers, his mouth opening and claiming her—

Woof! Woof! Woof!

Cassie jumped at the sound of Luna's bark, and before she knew what was happening, the dog's leash slipped out of her hand and Luna ran toward a person who was walking by on the beach. As she went after the dog, she put a hand up to shield her eyes from the sun.

"Hey, Luna," said a familiar voice. "What are you doing here, girl?"

Cassie froze as she watched Logan squat down and grab the leash, securing her dog. Then he scratched Luna's ears and gently roughed up her fur as he played with her.

Still dazed after being pulled so abruptly from the daydream, all she could think was *Well, total Logan immersion didn't work.*

Now, she wasn't just thinking about him—he was standing here in front of her.

Since Luna, the little traitor, had announced herself, there was nowhere for Cassie to hide. Even if she could disappear into the dunes, what good would it do to hide? She'd have to face him sooner or later.

The best defense was a good offense. She needed to hit this head-on.

"Are you following me?" she called as she walked toward him.

He got to his feet.

"I could ask you the same thing," he said. "This is the third time today we've ended up in the same place."

He cracked the hint of a smile.

Okay, he didn't seem too weirded out over the kiss.

"I think my dog likes you more than she likes me."

She reached out for the leash.

"Yeah? Well, rumor has it I'm pretty irresistible. Women have been known to spontaneously kiss me."

She groaned and fought the urge to cover her face with her hands. "Yeah, about that. I'm sorry. I didn't mean to put you on the spot."

He waved away her apology.

"You surprised me. I don't do well with surprises. Do you want to take a walk?"

"Sure."

"Full disclosure, after you left, I went back into the conference room to get my things. I looked out the window and saw you down on the beach. After I had a second to digest the situation, I realized you might be on to something. So, I came down here to see if I could catch you and we could talk about things."

"So, you *are* following me." She gave his arm a playful push.

"Guilty as charged."

She slanted a glance at him and saw a muscle tick in his jaw.

"Dalton seems determined to have his way. Maybe the best way out of this is through it. In other words, what if we let him make our so-called chemistry bit a part of the show?"

Her stomach flip-flopped.

"Are you comfortable with that?" she asked. "I

mean, I've gotten the distinct feeling that you don't even want to be on the show."

She stole another glance at him and saw his shoulders rise and fall. "Honestly, I don't want to be on the show. I don't even want to be back in Tinsley Cove, but I'm here. For reasons I can't get into, this show means a lot to my mom."

"Your whole family is here. Why don't you want to be back in Tinsley Cove?"

As soon as the words left her mouth, she realized she shouldn't have said *whole family*.

"And that was so insensitive of me," she added. "I realize your late wife was your family, too. Is she the reason it's hard for you to be here?"

He slanted a glance at her.

"Actually, yes. Natalie and I both grew up here. Everywhere I look there's a memory. Her family is here, too."

"Do you get along with them?"

When he didn't answer right away, she said, "Look, I'm sorry. I don't mean to pry."

"It's okay. Natalie and I met in elementary school. We were together for so long that I don't know what they'd think if they saw me moving on after all that's happened."

"But it's been almost five years," she said. "You're young. Surely they don't expect you to put yourself on a shelf for the rest of your life. Do they?"

"It's probably more me than it is them. It's complicated. I haven't seen them since Natalie's funeral. I need to go by and see them and tell them what's going on. I believe they don't even know we're filming. I'll reach out and tell them."

"You haven't seen them in five years?"

He shook his head. "They live here. I've been in California this whole time. But the anniversary is coming up and I'm here now…"

The wind swallowed his words.

She waited for him to say more, but he didn't. There was so much more to this than he was saying. She had so many questions. For once in her life, she caught herself before she put her foot in her mouth and asked one too many questions.

"What about you?" he asked. "Are you still in touch with your ex-in-laws?"

"Nope. My ex got them and the house in the divorce. It only stands to reason, since his folks gave us the house as a wedding present. But let's just suffice to say that there's no love lost between them and me."

She didn't like dredging up the past any more than he seemed to. So she changed the subject while she had the chance.

"So how do you want to play this?" Cassie asked.

"I guess we just play it by ear and see where things go. If that's okay with you."

"Sounds like a plan." Because what else was she supposed to say?

"Why don't we exchange phone numbers?" he

suggested. "We can see how things work tomorrow. Maybe once we get a feel for the storyline that Dalton is trying to form, then we can be proactive and come up with narratives that will direct it so that it feels most natural to us."

Cassie called her phone with Logan's cell so that they had each other's numbers, and then they said goodbye.

She was just walking into the bungalow when her phone buzzed with a text message.

Hey, it's Logan. Good talk, but forgot to say...
You were right. The kiss wasn't so bad.
$Fuel + O_2 \rightarrow CO_2 + H_2O$
See you tomorrow.

She read the text again.

Or at least most of it.

It took her a minute to read beyond *The kiss wasn't so bad*, because she kept reading that part over and over. A few times she even read it out loud, just to make sure she was reading it right and wasn't reading more into it than was there.

Well, she probably was reading too much into it. Even so, the thought made her shiver, and she crossed her arms and rubbed her arm with her free hand.

That's when she realized that the house was blessedly cooler than when she'd left for the meeting this morning. The air-conditioning was working. Thank you, Sophie!

Even if she'd had a rocky start in Tinsley Cove, maybe things were finally sorting themselves out.

She glanced at the text again.

But what in the world did *Fuel* + $O_2 \rightarrow CO_2$ + H_2O mean?

Science had never been her strong suit, but recalling what she could of basic chemistry, she knew that CO_2 was the symbol for carbon dioxide, and H_2O was the symbol for water...

"Does CO_2 + H_2O stand for soda water?" she asked Luna.

The dog tilted her head to the side.

"Yeah, I don't think so, either, because there's also that part about *Fuel* + $O_2 \rightarrow$ part. *Hmm*...which is a puzzle, Luna. Just like Logan."

On a whim she pulled up the search engine on her phone and looked up: what does Fuel + $O_2 \rightarrow$ CO_2 + H_2O mean.

She gasped when answer turned up: Fuel + $O_2 \rightarrow$ CO_2 + H_2O is the chemical equation for complete combustion reaction.

Chapter Six

Call Sheet
Production: *Selling Sandcastle*
Date: Tuesday, June 6
General Crew Call: 7:00 a.m.
First Shooting Call: 8:30 a.m.
Lunch: 12:00 p.m.
Location(s): Sandcastle Real Estate office; Broadhurst House—Seahorse Island
Set & Scene Description(s): Office interior— front desk and Bert McFadden's office. Broad- hurst House interior and exterior.

Cast/Call Time/Location:
Bert McFadden—8:30 a.m./Sandcastle Real Estate office

Logan McFadden—8:30 a.m./Sandcastle Real
Estate office
Lucy McFadden (featured extra)—8:30 a.m./
Sandcastle Real Estate office
Cassie Houston—9:00 a.m./Sandcastle Real
Estate office
Bunny McFadden—10:30 a.m./Sandcastle Real
Estate office—cast photo
Forest McFadden—10:30 a.m./Sandcastle Real
Estate office—cast photo
Owen McFadden—10:30 a.m./Sandcastle Real
Estate office—cast photo
Logan McFadden—3:00 p.m./Sandcastle Real
Estate office—Broadhurst House—Seahorse
Island
Cassie Houston—3:00 p.m./Sandcastle Real
Estate office—Broadhurst House—Seahorse
Island

On Tuesday morning, the cameras started rolling
about a half hour after Logan arrived at the Sandcastle Real Estate office. The scene Dalton wanted
to film made it appear that Logan was just arriving
at the office. So, when they were ready to roll, he
had to go back outside and enter through the front
door again.

"Welcome back," chirped Logan's cousin Lucy
McFadden from her post at the front desk. "You were
gone long enough, dude. We missed you."

Her bright-eyed eagerness made Logan smile. Last night, Dalton had issued an urgent call for someone to occupy the Sandcastle Real Estate front desk so that the office appeared *higher end*. Logan supposed that a receptionist elevated a business. As far back as he could remember, each person had always handled their own calls, or during busy times family members had taken turns doing front-desk duty, where they welcomed walk-ins and fielded phone calls on a rotating basis.

Dalton seemed intent on portraying them as something they weren't.

Whatever.

Lucy, who seemed to have stars in her eyes, had been eager to drop everything and help. She was only twenty. Who could blame her for wanting to be on television, even if she was in the background?

Whatever made her happy.

This morning, Logan's task was to convincingly pretend he was having it out with his father for hiring Cassie without consulting him, which was ridiculous. However, yesterday, after his surprise encounter with Cassie, he'd realize that he needed to be a team player. He didn't have to like it, but he was here for his mom, so he needed to make the best of it. Just push through the nonsense and make it to the end. His mom would get her wish.

If he'd been more flexible with Natalie...maybe she'd still be here.

His heart ached like it was in a vise. So he shook off the memory and refocused on the future.

Maybe he'd find a way to steer the narrative of Dalton's circus in a more natural direction. In the meantime, he had to pretend to have a beef with his dad.

"Thanks, Lucy. I hear big changes were afoot while I was away."

She nodded, and her curly dark hair bobbed. She was the daughter of his uncle Brian—his father's younger brother, who owned a car dealership in Tinsley Cove.

"Is Dad in?" Logan asked.

"Cut!" called Dalton.

What the hell?

Logan took a deep breath and turned toward Dalton, trying not to let his irritation show.

Not only was Dalton the executive producer, but he was also directing. Clearly, when you owned the production company, you could assume as many roles as you wanted.

"Logan, what would you think of calling him Bert rather than Dad?" Dalton asked.

"You want me to call my father by his first name?"

"Yeah, why not? Since there are four McFadden offspring, there's going to be a whole lot of *Dad this* and *Dad that* going on around here. If you address him by his name, it will break up the monotony."

"I thought the point of this show was that it's a family-owned business, and a mother, father and the four offspring, as you put it, are the featured players. It stands to reason that there would be a lot of *Dad this* and *Dad that* flying around."

"Yeah, so let's have you call him Bert."

Logan gritted his teeth. "Are you asking me if I want to call him Bert or are you telling me to do it?"

Dalton smiled and pointed finger guns at Logan. "I knew you'd be a quick study. Let's consider it done."

"You might want clue him in, because he going to have a strange reaction since I usually don't address him by his first name."

"I'm good with whatever works," Bert called from his office.

Logan sighed. He was tempted to ask, with so much *scripting* to the point of altering reality, why didn't they hire actors to play the roles and call it a drama? But then Cassie walked through the front door.

Their gazes snagged.

She smiled.

Logan's mouth went dry, and he forgot the question.

"Okay, let's pick it up from your last line, Logan," Dalton said. "Action."

"Is *Bert* in?" Logan asked Lucy.

He emphasized the name. It felt strange in his mouth.

Logan half expected Dalton to call cut, but he carried on.

"Of course he is. Does he ever leave?" Lucy chuckled. "He's in his office. Would you like me to buzz him?"

"No, thanks. I'd rather surprise him."

Lucy nodded. "Suit yourself."

Out of the corner of his eye, Logan could see Cassie following behind the film crew as they tracked him down the hallway. Realizing she was watching him made him hyper-aware. Since Dalton didn't stop the action, Logan walked through the open door into his father's office.

"Good morning, Bert," he said.

Apparently, playing into the drama they were tasked to create, Bert didn't look up from the newspaper he was reading.

Logan lowered himself onto the chair in front of his father's desk, wishing his dad—*err, Bert*—would add to the dialogue.

"Cut!" Dalton yelled. "Logan, remember you're angry, because you've just learned that Bert cut you out of the hiring process. Resentment is simmering like a fireball in the pit of your stomach. We need to see that."

Logan ran a hand through his hair and cleared his throat.

Resentment was simmering, but not toward his dad.

"I'm not sure what you want me to do." Logan shrugged. "Even if there is a so-called problem between us, we're not going to come to blows. That's not how we handle things."

Dalton stroked his chin. "Okay, how would you play it? What would Logan McFadden do?"

"I would keep my cool, because if... *Bert* had done something that made me resentful—something that might pit me against my family—I would talk it out with him. If that's too civil for you, doesn't it stand to reason that if I lose my cool, wouldn't it just prove that he was justified in his decision to cut me out of the business decision?"

"*Hmm*..." Dalton said, rubbing his chin again, as if Logan had just proposed a complex problem. "Okay, maybe we need to up the stakes here. Forest and Owen both hold the title of vice president, but you don't—"

"That's because it's been a while since I've worked for Sandcastle."

"Right. I did some digging and discovered that your company, McFadden Construction, went belly up three years ago."

Logan's eye started twitching. Had he not made it clear that his past was off-limits?

"That would be good motivation for Bert not to make you a partner. He's not quite convinced of your business sense or your commitment to Sandcastle Real Estate. He wants you to prove yourself. He needs you to show him why you're valuable to this company. Prove that he can trust you even though you failed in your own business."

The words were a punch in the gut.

"What part of 'my past is off-limits' don't you understand? I'm serious. Dalton, I'm giving you what I can, but if you can't respect boundaries, then…"

"Then what?" Dalton asked.

Logan didn't answer. He wanted to say he would walk away, but that would upset his mom. Instead, he and Dalton engaged in a stare down until Dalton finally blinked.

"Okay, everyone, let's take ten minutes to regroup. We'll pick up from Logan entering Bert's office."

Logan reached up and pulled off the microphone that the production crew had wired to him. He tossed it onto the chair where he'd been sitting. Dalton was already huddled with Bert, giving him notes, but as Logan left the office, Dalton called, "Logan, truce, man. Okay? We're getting there. This is the emotion I need from you. Just channel it into the feud with your dad."

Logan kept walking straight out the front door and past the camera that was stationed outside. He was getting into his truck when Cassie called, "Logan, wait. Please."

Logan stopped, his hand on the open door.

"Are you okay?" she asked.

"I'm fine." His voice sounded anything but fine.

"Where are you going?" she asked. He followed

her gaze to the trailer emblazoned with the Top Drawer Productions logo that was parked horizontally across the entrance to the office's parking lot. Even though the official announcement had yet to go out and the cast and crew had been sworn to secrecy until that happened, it hadn't stopped Dalton from creating a spectacle.

"To sit in my truck."

"Want to take a walk instead?" Cassie asked. "I thought I'd see if I could find a place that sells gum."

When Logan didn't answer, Cassie said, "Just a short walk, since we have to be back in approximately eight and a half minutes."

"You're going to chew gum on camera?" he asked. "Something tells me Dalton will flip out."

She nodded and smiled mischievously. "Maybe his head will explode. That would be fun, but full disclosure, I don't really want gum. It sounded better than saying I want breath mints, which might make you think I have bad breath."

He laughed. Then his mind raced back to the kiss they'd shared yesterday. She didn't have bad breath. She'd tasted good—fresh—like mint and sunshine and something delicious. And since that kiss was meant purely to break the ice, he knew he shouldn't be thinking about the word *delicious*.

Actually, he shouldn't be thinking about it at all.

"So, you grew up with Dalton, didn't you?"

Logan gave a half nod, half shrug. "We both grew

up in Tinsley Cove. He's a few years older, my brother Forest's age."

"So, y'all didn't hang out?"

"Hell no, he's always been a prick."

Cassie startled, and Logan wished he'd kept the sentiment to himself.

Though, in Logan's book, Dalton Hart would forever and always be a prick, because he'd tried to date Natalie when he knew damn good and well she'd been too young for him and she and Logan were committed.

"I'm beginning to wonder if Dalton hired you to babysit me," Logan said.

"Babysit?" She pulled a face and shook her head. "A babysitter is the last thing you need, Logan."

He cocked a brow at her. "Oh, yeah? What exactly is it that you think I need?"

She bit her bottom lip and looked him up and down.

She smiled and shook her head and started walking toward Main Street. Logan closed the truck door and followed after her.

"We only have about six minutes left, so we probably won't have time to buy gum, but let's take that walk anyway," she said.

"You didn't answer my question," he said when he caught up with her.

"I know."

They walked around the production trailer, which

was attracting attention, as evidenced by the knot of bystanders clustered on the sidewalk.

"Are we still supposed to keep this show under wraps?" Cassie whispered. "Has Dalton released anything to the press yet?"

"I have no idea. He's from this town, and he knows how nosy people can be and how easily rumors can start. So, if he is going to create a spectacle in the parking lot, it's his problem."

"Logan McFadden, is that you?" called a woman about Logan's age. "Hey, it's Lindy Hendrickson. Do you remember me? Natalie and I were friends in high school."

There was a heaviness in Logan's chest. "I do remember you," he said. "Good to see you, Lindy. I hate to run—we're on an errand, and we need to be back in five minutes."

"We're all curious about what's going on in there," she said.

Logan shrugged. "I was wondering the same thing."

Lindy frowned. "Weren't you just inside?"

"I was. It's a circus in there."

Lindy's brows knitted. Clearly, it wasn't the inside scoop she'd hoped to get from Logan. Her gaze slid from him to Cassie, and she made a slow appraisal of Cassie before returning to him. Since Logan wouldn't tell her what was going on, she'd probably form her own conclusion.

For a moment, he worried that word would get back to Natalie's family that he had been seen in town with *a woman*. To preempt this, he considered introducing Cassie and explaining that she was his colleague. But just as quickly, he decided against it.

It was none of their damn business. He didn't owe anyone an explanation.

He'd pay a call to Bob and Lorraine Holmes tonight or tomorrow…as soon as he could. His heart ached at the prospect of trying to explain to them why he hadn't kept in touch since Natalie's funeral. He just…

He couldn't.

Without another word, he and Cassie bypassed the crowd and walked down Main Street. They would have just enough time to take a right on Formosa Avenue and circle back around to the office and come in the back door.

Back in the office, Cassie watched from the sidelines as Dalton called quiet on the set and began filming Logan and Bert's big confrontation scene.

After their walk, Logan seemed to be more amenable to giving Dalton what he wanted. That was a good thing, because Dalton seemed to have a will of iron.

The first action had Bert sitting behind his desk. He lowered the newspaper he'd been reading and scrutinized his son.

"What do you want, Logan?"

Ebenezer Scrooge couldn't have been colder.

She saw Logan flinch. It was almost impercepti-
ble, but she saw it and it confirmed that this wasn't
the Bert McFadden she'd come to know. It seemed
to be exactly what Dalton wanted.

"When were you going to tell me that you've hired
someone?" Logan's voice sounded void of emotion.

"You'll meet her at the staff meeting in about—"
Bert checked his Rolex. "Twenty minutes or so."

Logan locked gazes with his father.

Bert's right brow shot up, a subtle warning: *don't
challenge me.*

It gave Cassie chills. She hoped Bert would have
a chance to show his real personality and not this
steely, all-business hardnose.

"What else?" Bert asked.

"Forest and I are going to share the Broadhurst
House listing," Logan said. "It's the fifteen-million-
dollar beachfront home on Seahorse Island."

Bert shrugged, clearly unimpressed.

"It's a start," he said. "You'll need to work hard
if you're going to keep up."

Logan's fingers drummed a one-two-three ca-
dence on his thigh.

"Of course, you can count on it."

Logan's discomfort was palpable, and Cassie
wanted to yell, *Cut! This isn't how they are.*

"Of course, Cassie could give you a run for your money."

"The new hire?" Logan asked flatly. "I thought you brought her in to stage our listings?"

"Why would I hire a one-trick pony? She's going to get her real estate license."

I am?

She glanced at Dalton, but he was absorbed in the scene between Logan and Bert.

Um...okay. Nice of you to let me know.

Uh-oh. Were they going to use this as another point of drama and contention? Because she didn't know the first thing about getting a real estate license.

Cassie and Troy had eloped less than two months after her mom died. Saying his parents weren't thrilled was putting it mildly. Even so, she'd been Troy's wife, and they'd tolerated her.

They paid for his college tuition, but she and Troy were on their own when it came to her education. Really, she had never expected them to pay for her. So, she took a class at a time—whatever they could afford without taking out student loans—and worked at the family furniture store.

Soon it became too easy to skip semesters here and there. Five years ago, she ended up dropping out. At twenty-two, Troy and her peers were graduating, but she hadn't even accumulated enough credits to get her AA degree.

That was fine with her. She was married and madly in love. While she and Troy weren't wealthy, they had been financially secure working at his parents' furniture store. Troy had a business degree and would take over the business in due time. She didn't have a passion about anything but being Troy's wife. So, why spend the time and money?

Now, she could kick herself.

"Cassie is ambitious," Bert said.

I am? I mean, okay. If Bert can play the ballbuster, I can play ambitious. I hope.

"As I said, Cassie Houston is going to give you a run for your money," Bert continued. "Watch your back, son. On that note, what else do you have for me?"

Oh, no. A sinking feeling, like a rock that had been thrown into a deep well, rippled in her stomach.

Logan mentioned some leads. *Go, Logan.*

"You'll get a full report soon," he said.

Bert made a disappointed sound in his throat. "Make sure it's sooner rather than later. And speaking of reports, I have a staff meeting to run in a few minutes. I'm counting on you to be there to welcome Cassie to the Sandcastle family."

Chapter Seven

After only two days, Logan decided that the best way to appease Dalton was to nod at his over-the-top suggestions and then find a way around them.

For example, after Dalton had insisted that Logan call his dad by his first name, Logan simply avoided addressing his father by name.

The same went for the staged staff meeting where Bert "introduced" Cassie to the Sandcastle crew on camera. Logan was supposed to take issue with his father—err, Bert—hiring someone without consulting him. After the introduction, Logan welcomed her, then did his best to fade into the background, letting everyone else talk.

There was no scowling or confrontation or mustache twirling like a subversive cartoon villain plotting to overthrow his nemesis.

The best part was that Dalton didn't seem to notice when Logan withdrew, which was perfect.

He was learning that a "scripted" show could easily go off script and if Dalton was happy with it, it became the new direction.

The big drama at the staff meeting had focused on Cassie joining the team and hitting the ground running. Bert revealed that she only had a day and a half to stage a seven-thousand-square-foot mansion in time for a photographer that had already been booked. Bert drove home the fact that if the listing wasn't staged and photographed so it could be shown to prospective buyers by the end of the day Thursday, the homeowner was prepared to change real estate firms.

In what world would that really happen?

Bert had put Cassie in touch with Stephan Baxter from Baxter and Mason Fine Furniture.

The company had a warehouse in Hainesville, which wasn't too far from Tinsley Cove.

Stephan Baxter was a longtime family friend. He'd come to all the parties Logan's folks were so fond of throwing—holiday get-togethers, New Year's parties, football tailgating and other soirees for no reasons. Stephan and his business partner, Chip Mason, had always been on the guest list.

Before their mother had gotten sick, their parents

had been talking about having Bunny use Baxter and Mason furniture to stage Sandcastle Real Estate's higher-end listings. The furniture would be loaned on a consignment basis, with the intention of buyers taking the house lock, stock and barrel, and they would negotiate a package price for the furniture. After Bunny got sick, the plan had been put on the back burner, and they hadn't revisited it.

After a phone call from Bert, Baxter was eager to rekindle the plan. Not only did it mean another avenue in which Baxter and Mason could sell their furniture, but Bert had also negotiated a promotional credit and promised they would try to mention the company every chance they could.

Since Bert had gotten the green light for the furniture, he had tasked Cassie with staging Sandcastle's brand-new listing, the luxury coastal estate Broadhurst House on Seahorse Island, in a day and a half. Part of the rush was designed to give Dalton the ticking-clock drama he craved, but in reality, a photographer had been scheduled to photograph the place on Thursday.

Never mind that the photos could've been rescheduled. There was no time like the present.

After Bert made introductions by phone, Cassie wanted to go to the Baxter and Mason warehouse to get an idea of what was available before they filmed her looking at Broadhurst House to decide how to furnish it.

Since Cassie was new to the area and they were scheduled to film together at Broadhurst House that afternoon, Logan offered to drive her. Why not? Broadhurst House was located thirty minutes outside Tinsley Cove, and the warehouse was halfway in between the two.

These days, his truck seemed like a safe place where he didn't have to worry about cameras or production people eavesdropping on conversations.

Bottom line, offering to drive just seemed like the decent thing to do, since he would be driving right by the warehouse anyway.

He turned on the stereo, and the music streaming service he subscribed to began playing a random daily mix that was supposedly custom made for him based on the music he listened to.

"If you don't mind me asking," Cassie said, "is Broadhurst House your listing or... I mean, clearly, if we're staging it, it's Sandcastle Real Estate's listing. I don't mean to be nosy. I'm just trying to learn the lingo and who does what."

He didn't blame her for asking. They were getting so much thrown at them so fast that it was hard to keep things straight. The last thing either of them wanted was to look like a fool on television. He'd like to think that Dalton wouldn't want that, either, since it could reflect badly on the show, but these days it seemed like nothing was normal.

"Originally, the listing belonged to my brother

Forest. Since he's busy with his mayoral campaign and I'm restarting with Sandcastle Real Estate, Forest and the homeowners have agreed to let me co-list."

"That sounds like a good arrangement," Cassie said.

"I guess so. It means I'll be doing most of the legwork to sell the place while Forest campaigns. But whatever."

He slanted a quick glance at her and was struck by her natural beauty. So, he redirected his attention to the street in front of him, keeping his eyes on the road where they should be.

Even Cassie recognized the good in the arrangement with Forest, it meant he and Forest would split the commission once the place sold, but it also meant that Logan would see a payday sooner than if he had to find and sell his own listing. The place was listed for $15 million. According to Forest and their father, Seahorse Island was a hot market. Property was selling quickly and above asking price.

Every commission he made would put him that much closer to paying off the rest of the debt that Natalie had left behind. After he did that, he would be in a better place to reestablish himself.

Now that he had some time and distance, he knew he couldn't blame Natalie for his business failing. Sure, there had been a lot of debt, with the medical bills and other things…but the truth was that after losing his wife, he'd shut down. He would've been happier if they'd buried him right beside her. He'd let everything go. He'd lost their house, lost his business and basically lost his will to live.

Then his mom had gotten sick, and it had been the jolt he'd needed to get his sorry ass in gear. Losing Natalie—and the way it had played out in the end—still hurt like a mother, but at least he had the good sense to realized he wasn't doing anyone any good wallowing in his own pain. Least of all his own mother. Even though she lived on the other side of the country—or maybe because there was that much distance between them—she had been worried sick over him.

He could be a selfish bastard, but even he knew that Bunny needed to focus all her energy on getting well, and she couldn't do that if she was fretting about him.

In his peripheral vision, he saw Cassie shift in the passenger seat, angling her body toward him. He could feel the weight of her gaze on him as he drove.

"This is a dangerous trip," she said.

"Why? Do you not like the way I drive?"

"Don't be ridiculous." She laughed. "We're going to a furniture store, and I'd love to buy some new furniture, but I can't. That's why it's a dangerous trip."

"Why not?" he asked. "Why not treat yourself?"

"It's not exactly in the budget. So, you have to promise me you won't let me buy anything."

"I'll do my best, but I'm not exactly the boss of you. I'm not going to tie you up or anything."

She made a suggestive noise, and he was sorry he'd said the part about tying her up.

"I know, it's not your responsibility to make me exercise good judgment. I've learned the hard way, so you'd think that would be enough to keep me from making the same mistake again."

He had to admit he was curious about what she meant. Money? Repeating mistakes? He flashed back to the argument he and Natalie had the day of her accident. Themes were repeating.

That familiar sick feeling tried to drag him into the black hole, but he fended it off.

"Since Top Drawer is paying for my lodging for three months, my expenses are relatively low. I have vowed to save eighty percent of what I'm making on the show. You see, I should've put away the money I made while I was married and working at my ex-in-laws' furniture store, but I didn't."

"Did you buy furniture?"

"No. I bought clothes. I'm kind of addicted to clothes and shoes."

So was Natalie. The memory felt like fingers tearing out his heart. He put the memory into a box, mentally slammed the lid shut and shoved it into the way back of his mind.

"We didn't have a mortgage, because Troy's family gave us a house as a wedding present. Well, they gave him the house, because they never liked me—"

"What's wrong with them?" Logan asked. "How could they not like you?"

She reached over and squeezed his arm.

"Troy also had a trust fund, which meant that we had no debt and low expenses. So, I looked at what I made as pocket money and I spent it."

"You spent the money you made. It's not like you racked up a bunch of debt, right?"

"Of course not. No, no, no. I am allergic to debt. But my sister, Gabby, pointed out one day that if I'd saved even some of what I made rather than squandering it on clothes, I might have a pretty nice down payment for a house. Now, it's going to take me a while to pay rent and save up a chunk of change. That's why, even though I will probably want to buy furniture, I can't buy anything."

"Hold on, how long were you married?"

"Seven years."

"This guy was from a wealthy family and you didn't get any sort of settlement?"

"No. I wasn't in it for the money. I loved him, but as I said, Troy's parents never liked me. They set up everything in a trust so I couldn't touch it."

He stole a glance at her and found she was staring out the passenger side window. Her neck was long and looked delicate, and he had to fight the urge to tuck a strand of hair behind her ear and tell her that if they didn't like her, they were jackasses. But the words couldn't launch off his tongue. He ended up swallowing them and keeping both hands on the wheel...where they belonged.

"Yeah, his parents were pretty snooty," she said. "I always felt this pressure to be the best I could be. Or probably to be someone else who wasn't me. I thought if I always dressed well and worked hard for them, someday they might grow to love me. But ha! The joke was on me. Looking back, I realize I used shopping to fill this emptiness inside me that came on after my mom died."

Since her mom died.

He thought about asking how her father's death had affected her, but it felt too personal.

Plus, the box of grief and misery that he'd shoved away suddenly sprang open, and all sorts of questions about Natalie jumped out. Had his wife shopped to fill a similar emptiness? Had he been so hell-bent on success that he couldn't see the problems that led to her death gathering like angry storm clouds?

Had he been that self-absorbed and blind to her needs?

He vaguely recalled that Cassie had asked him a question, but he hadn't heard it because he'd been in his head. Case in point for blind and self-absorbed.

"Hello! Earth to Logan," Cassie said. "Where'd ya go there, buddy?"

"Sorry," he said. "What were you saying?"

"I'm sorry if I'm boring you. But you seriously almost missed out. I was asking about your favorite kind of cookie."

"You're not boring me, but you want to know my *what*?" He slanted a quick glance at her and saw the earnestness on her face start to fade to confusion.

"Your favorite cookie?" she said. "Please tell me you do know what a cookie is."

"Of course I do. It was a random question. Kind of a non sequitur."

"Maybe on whatever planet your mind had sailed off to, but in my world, any time is a good time for a talk about cookies."

"Why do you want to know?" he asked. "Is it some kind of psychological test? You know, you evaluate my personality based on the answer to a random question?"

"Um, I have no idea what that means, but are you always so cynical? I wasn't trying to invade your privacy or get inside your head. I'm asking because I wanted to bake you some cookies to thank you for coming to my rescue when I was locked out. But heaven forbid you think I'm trying to psychoanalyze you based on your choice of cookie. I mean, is that even a thing? Even if it was, I wouldn't—"

"Peanut butter," he said.

"Oh," she said. "Really? Me, too. I love peanut butter cookies and I have *the best* recipe. Just you wait and see. When I worked at my ex-in-laws' furniture store, I would always bake cookies when we had sales. You know, I wanted to add a special touch. There's something so homey about fresh-baked cookies. They just always make you feel so welcome and loved. And you know what? I would always bake a batch of chocolate chip and a batch of my special peanut butter cookies, and hands down, the peanut butter cookies would always disappear first. I got to the point where I printed the recipe on the back of my business card because invariably people would ask for it. Actually, though, it wasn't really a business card. I had to get special cards made—they were recipe cards, because, well, you can't exactly fit a whole recipe on the back of a traditional business card, and I didn't really have a business card since I just staged the furniture for them."

"You like to talk, don't you?" He didn't mean for his words to sound so accusatory.

She gasped. "Rude."

Yeah, he supposed it was, though he hadn't meant it that way.

"Sorry," he said. "What I meant was you and I are different. You seem to process things out loud, and I...don't."

"Yeah, you're pretty laconic, aren't you?"

He smiled. "Laconic? That's a good one. I've been called a lot of things, but I think *laconic* is the nicest way anyone ever put it."

She laughed. "What have people called you?"

"Moody, irritable, sullen, arrogant…"

"That's not very nice," she said.

He shrugged. "What's that saying? If the shoe fits?"

"It's still not very nice. I don't think you're arrogant. I don't know you well enough yet to know your moods or what irritates you. Unless too much talking annoys you?"

He stopped at a red light and stole a glance at her. Her wide green eyes looked like the ocean on a sunny day.

"I do talk a lot, don't I?" she said. "And you don't have to answer that, because you've already said it. My ex-husband used to say, 'Cassie, take a breath.'"

She stopped midsentence and pressed her fingers to her lips.

"And that's all I'm going to say."

She clamped her mouth shut and pretended to turn a lock on her lips and throw away the key.

They rode in silence for a while, but he couldn't stop thinking about her husband telling her to take a breath. That was rude and belittling, though it wasn't his place to say it. He and Natalie had argued like all married couples, but he'd never stooped to personal insults.

The hands of guilt wrapped around his solar plexus and squeezed, reminding him that he didn't deserve to feel superior to anyone—especially a man he'd never met.

Because of him, Natalie was dead.

That was worse than any backhanded insult.

As if underscoring that fact, the intro to the Rascal Flatts song "What Hurts the Most" sounded through the speakers.

In his mind, Logan saw Natalie slam the car door. This song had been blaring as she gunned the engine and backed out of the driveway—

No!

He reached out and turned off the radio.

When Logan drove down the cobblestone driveway and parked under Broadhurst House's majestic portico, Cassie could tell the house was special. It possessed a timeless old-world charm, despite the fact that it had been built in the 1990s. Even so, thanks to the luxurious European finishes, the place stood out from the colorful beach houses on the island.

The Rascal Flatts song had sent Logan back into his shell. After he'd turned off the radio, they'd ridden in silence. He hadn't seemed like he wanted to talk about it, and she hadn't asked. Even though she liked to talk, she knew when to be quiet.

Logan unlocked the arched gothic-style wooden front door and kept his hand on the ornate wrought iron handle.

"See this?" He lifted his hand and ran it along the weathered, time-worn wood. "The door is made of oak. It dates back to early 1800s. It's from an old Irish church. All the hardware—the wrought iron hinges and door bolts—is original, made by a nineteenth-century blacksmith. Or so claims the write-up that Forest gave me."

"Huh." Cassie furrowed her brow and stepped closer to examine the door, happy to meet him on common ground. "I wonder if the door is new. I mean, I know it's old, you just said that, but I wonder if it's newly installed. I would think wood—especially antique wood—might not be the best choice for the humid salt air."

Logan raised his brows and nodded. "I wondered the same thing." He ran his hand over the door again. "It feels like there's some kind of sealant on it."

She tracked the motion of his big, strong-looking hand as it traced the wood grain and wondered what it would feel like on her body. Then she wondered where in the world that thought had come from, because…because she had no business buying in to the fake-chemistry bit that they were supposed to be selling to the television audience. Clearly, he was still carrying around a load of baggage after losing his wife. And they were just so different in every way. But the bottom line was this quirky job that had fallen into her lap could be the new start she so desperately needed. A chance to finally get herself together and figure out her place in the world. Because it was high time she figured it out and got on with her life.

"It is what it is, and there's no mistaking that this place is a showstopper. Let's go look at the rest of the house."

Silently, she and Logan made their way through the large, empty home, their footfalls sounding on the marble floors and echoing in the expanse of the lofty ceilings.

Even unfurnished, the house was like something from a dream. It boasted breathtaking views of the water from every room. There was a swimming pool, a hot tub, an elevator, a gourmet kitchen, a movie theater and a billiard room, and that was just scratching the surface. The stunning seven-thou-sand-square-foot, eight-bedroom home was like a castle, Cassie thought.

"This place is gorgeous," she mused. "If I lived here, I might never leave the compound. Of course, with this much square footage, I would probably get lost and spend the first six months wandering from room to room trying to find my way out. But if I could live in a place like this, that's a chance I'm willing to take."

Logan nodded.

"How are you going to sell it?" she asked.

He ran his hand through his hair. "I guess I need to figure that out pretty fast."

After surveying the first two floors, they found

the primary suite on the third floor. It took up the entire level with its lounge area, his and hers walk-in closets, and dual vanity with bathroom opening onto a private balcony that overlooked a serene marshy waterway. It was so peaceful up here, looking down on the Broadhurst kingdom.

She could see the pool and patio area and the surrounding mature landscaping that looked like a private park...a park that led down to the water and dock with boat lift.

"See that path?" Logan pointed, and she followed his finger. "It leads to the beach. It's just a short walk. Basically, if you keep following it, it goes around the entire island."

"For fifteen million, I'd hope it would include a path."

He surprised her with a smile.

That's more like it.

As they stood side by side, a soft, briny breeze blew in from the water, and Cassie tipped her face up and breathed in deeply. This home was truly a one of a kind, and she was determined to stage it to showcase it at its best. Then the breeze stopped, and the enormity of the project set in.

"Thanks for taking me to the Baxter and Mason warehouse," she said.

"No problem. It was on the way."

While she'd talked to Stephan Baxter and they'd

gone over the pieces that were immediately available, Logan had roamed around solo. She'd imagined that he'd been processing the mood the song had thrown him into.

Maybe he was a moody guy? Everyone had their moments. He could also be considered a deep thinker. Troy had been moody, too. Actually, *petulant* was a better way to describe it.

"Can I ask you a question?" she said.

He looked at her warily. "Sure."

"That Rascal Flatts song seemed to upset you..."

"Yes."

"Do you want to talk about it?"

He stood there with his forearms braced on the balcony rail for a few silent beats. She forced herself not to say a word until he answered, which was a challenge, because she hated long, awkward stretches of silence. She was trying so hard to learn how to chill out and embrace the awkward rather than making it more awkward by filling it with nonsense.

Plus, the less she said, the more he would say.

Maybe.

"The night she died, that song was playing on the radio as she drove away. She'd cranked up the volume and—" His voice caught on the last word. He cleared his throat. "It's a trigger. I'm sorry you had to experience it."

Cassie reached out and put her hand on his arm.

"You don't have to apologize, and if you ever want

to talk about things, I'm a pretty good listener. Despite how you think I talk too much."

He offered that half smile of his, and his dimple winked at her, making the butterflies in her stomach flutter and then fly in formation.

"How long have you been divorced?" he asked. "You don't have to answer if that's too personal."

She waved her hand. "It's not... Well, I mean, it *is* personal—it's hard not to take it personally when your husband has an affair with your best friend. But *c'est la vie*. We've been divorced for just over two years now."

She forced a smile, because she didn't want him to see how much it still hurt.

"That sucks," he said. "I'm sorry it happened to you. That's a hell of a betrayal."

"What can you do? Divorce is no piece of cake, but I can't imagine what you've been going through. Losing someone you love. How long were you and your wife married?"

"Two years."

She sucked in a breath. "That's so unfair. You guys were still newlyweds. The woman you loved was taken from you. Fate separated you without giving you a choice. Troy and I had a choice, but he chose to throw our marriage away."

"Betrayal comes in all sorts of packages."

She turned and faced him. "What do you mean?"

He shook his head.

"It's a long, sad story. I don't want to burden you with it."

She put her hand on his. "You wouldn't be burdening me. I meant what I said—I'm here if you want to talk about it. Sometimes it helps to unload on an impartial third party."

He smiled at her. "Why? So you can psychoanalyze me?"

"What's with you and all this psychoanalysis talk? Maybe that's your subconscious screaming for help."

"Maybe it is."

He turned his hand over so that they were palm to palm.

"You're a good person, Cassie."

Her heart pounded at the feel of him. "Oh, well, I try."

Their hands lingered. He laced his fingers through hers and closed his hand, giving her a squeeze for the briefest moment. Then he flexed his fingers but left his hand under hers.

If she really wanted to let her mind go wild, she might believe he was trying it out, trying her on… seeing how they felt together, how they fit.

"Hello. Hello. Hello!" Dalton called from downstairs, breaking the spell. "Anybody here?"

Great. His timing was impeccable.

"Damn you, Dalton," Cassie whispered. "Go away."

Her hand, the one that had been on Logan's, flew to her mouth.

"That was supposed to be the quiet part," she said as heat scorched her cheeks. "Please pretend like I didn't say it out loud."

Chapter Eight

"It would be nice if more people said the quiet part out loud," Logan said.

Since Natalie had died, people—especially his own family—tended to tiptoe around him rather than talking about her. They didn't ask questions or mention her. Probably because they didn't want to upset him. Or maybe they just didn't know what to say.

"I thought you weren't a fan of talking," Cassie said.

He knew he'd put up his walls and he wasn't the most approachable person. Hell, until Cassie had asked, he hadn't even realized it wasn't such a bad thing to talk about Natalie.

It felt like his load had been lightened. He wasn't sure if it would be permanent.

"And on that note, we should get busy," he said.

He turned to go, but she shook her head.

"Wait," she whispered. "We don't have to go just yet. He doesn't even know we're up here, and the crew is still getting set up. Let's just hang out for a few more minutes."

Logan stopped and glanced around the empty room. "And do what?"

He hoped he hadn't misled her a moment ago by touching her hand. He'd meant it to be a friendly gesture. Or something like that. Hell, he had no idea what had been going through his head at that precise moment.

"I wanted to keep talking, since I have no idea when I'll catch you in such a chatty mood again."

She grinned at him and raised her brows.

"Okay," he said warily.

"Good, I have a question for you."

He grimaced, worrying that he might regret saying yes.

"In the meeting yesterday, your mom mentioned that you used to own your own contracting business?"

He nodded and watched the shadow of a date palm tree that was planted close to the balcony sweep the wall. He didn't really want to talk about it, because the way he lost the business made him sound like a loser.

"I was curious about it. It might come up in the course of filming, and I wanted to be prepared."

That wasn't a bad idea, to be proactive.

"Right after we moved to California, I started my own general contracting business. My folks had some contacts in the industry out there, and a client who was moving from the East Coast to the West wanted to build a house. I built that one, and it led to others."

"It sounds like it was going well. What happened?"

He inhaled long and slow and took his time exhaling.

"Let's just say things didn't work out the way I'd expected."

"Gotcha," she said. "If Dalton presses you, you can say that you've made a career change. General contracting isn't too far off from what you're doing now. You built houses, and now you're selling houses. I mean, it's not like you went into real estate after being in musical theater or something else out of left field."

A bark of laughter escaped his throat.

"Do I look the type who would be into musical theater?"

She smiled and shrugged. "I guess not. Unless

you can sing and dance? Maybe you have some hidden talents I don't know about."

He laughed and squinted at her as if she were insane. "Musical theater? Really? Talk about left field. No, I do not possess any hidden talents like that. In fact, it's more like what you see is what you get."

"Well, not gonna lie, I like what I see." She sounded husky and a little breathless, and if that hadn't jolted his guard back into place, Dalton walking into the room did.

"Here you two are," he said. "Didn't you hear me calling for you? I should've known I'd find you in the bedroom. How romantic."

In the workplace, Dalton's suggestive comments would win him a trip to the human resources office—at best. Logan made a mental note to ask Cassie if Dalton's pushing made her uncomfortable. Television show or no television show, he would put an end to it if she objected to the insinuations.

Jerk.

His gaze snared Cassie's, and judging by the look in her eyes, Logan was sure she was thinking something similar. Then again, she'd said the quiet part out loud.

It seemed like she was disappointed by the interruption.

Strangely, he was, too.

He liked how easy she was to talk to. He had to admit, he liked how her hand had felt in his.

The thought stirred something deep inside him that he hadn't felt in a long time. Though, he couldn't quite identify exactly what that feeling was. Even so, it was good to finally feel something again after all the years of feeling nothing.

"Cassie and I are discussing paint colors," Logan said, leading the conversation away from Dalton's bedroom talk. "What do you think, Cassie? Do you think we should do contrasting paint colors in the bedroom and the sitting room over there?"

"Good question." Her voice sounded a little over animated, but it might have just been Logan's own rush of adrenaline distorting his senses. No, the earlier huskiness that had lowered her voice when she'd said she liked what she saw was gone. It was replaced by an all-business tone.

"Dalton, Lucy reserved a painting crew for this afternoon." Cassie pulled her cell phone out of her pocket. "She texted me their number…here, let me find it."

She tapped her phone. "Got it. Logan, unless you prefer a specific color, I always used one called Parchment on the divider walls in the furniture store. It's neutral enough to go with everything, but it has more warmth than a basic white. I used to buy that stuff by the five-gallon drum and slap it on everything."

Logan shrugged. "Sounds good to me."

"Good," Cassie said. "We need to move fast if

we're going to get the walls painted before they deliver the furniture, which I still need to order. Ahh! I have so much to do."

Dalton frowned. "You guys are up here all alone and you're talking about paint and deadlines? You have to be two of the most boring individuals I've ever met."

"We have a job to do, Dalton," said Logan. "Not everything in the world is make-believe."

"Yeah, well, we're going to start filming you two looking over the house. Please try to bring some pizzazz."

Dalton rolled his eyes, threw a dismissive hand into the air and walked out of the room. As Cassie and Logan waited for the sound of Dalton's footfalls on the marble steps to fade, Cassie pressed both hands over her mouth to mute her laughter.

"Did he just give us the finger?" Cassie whispered after she'd recovered.

"Technically, no, but it conveyed the same sentiment."

"Nice, huh?" Cassie said. "I suppose we'd better get down there so we can film the scene."

As they walked down the three flights of steps to the ground-floor entryway, his thoughts ticked back to Cassie's divorce.

What kind of a man would be so weak as to cheat on someone like Cassie? And with her best friend, no less. What kind of a friend would betray someone who had trusted her? It must've been a punch to the gut. Natalie's death and the circumstances surrounding it had been soul crushing, and he still hadn't come to terms with the reality of it. At least he didn't have to deal with the added pain of knowing she'd betrayed their marriage with one of his friends.

Even so, he had enough guilt to live with. As if driving home the point, that familiar dull ache that resided in his chest pulsed even harder, reminding him that it was his fault. Natalie would still be here if not for him, so he had no business sticking his nose into anyone else's business.

"Any preference on furniture style or theme?" Cassie asked Logan as they stepped off the staircase and into the living room, where Dalton was barking out orders to the film crew as they set up.

"I defer to you, since you're the one with the good taste and the eye for design."

He was more of a big-picture person. He could tell her everything she wanted to know about coordinating and executing the construction of a project, but when it came to finishings and furnishings, that was a language he didn't speak.

"Thank you for your confidence in me," she said. "Since the fixtures and hardware have that delicious European feel and we won't have time to switch them out—and why would we do that, since they're so fab and they add value and uniqueness to the home?—

let's accentuate them with furniture that will look current while elevating the old-world vibe."

"I'll take your word for it," Logan said.

Cassie smiled.

"Very good," she said. "I need to call the painter to tell him the color, and then I have to get in touch with Stephan Baxter and place the order so they can deliver it tomorrow."

She blew out a breath before adding, "And we're sure they will come through on such short notice? That seems like a big ask."

Logan shrugged. "The photographer was booked before we knew we were going to dress this place up. If something happens, we're no worse off than we were before."

"That's a good way to look at it." This time she drew in a measured deep breath and nodded as she looked around. "I just want to do a good job."

A strange protective feeling washed over Logan.

"I know you do. If you do your part and they don't deliver, then it's on them."

His phone rang. When he looked at the screen, it was his mother. The earlier protectiveness for Cassie was edged out by a flash of concern. Since his mom had been sick every time she called—which wasn't often, especially since he'd been home—he worried that she was calling with more bad news. In the moments between the call coming in and his answering it, he gave himself a mental shake and remind himself if she was calling from her own phone, it wasn't so bad. It wasn't like Natalie's accident.

"Excuse me, I have to take this." He walked over to the living room's large wall of windows and answered.

"Hey."

"Logan, honey. It's Mom."

"Hi, Mom. What can I do for you?"

"I'm calling to invite you to dinner tonight. We're getting the entire family together. It's been so long since we've all been in town at the same time, I felt like celebrating. If it's all right with you, I'd like to invite Cassie, too."

A strange tangle of emotions bunched up in his stomach. He hoped it wouldn't be a night of more not-so-subtle attempts to push them together. Then he glanced back at Cassie and thought about her being new and alone in Tinsley Cove.

"Yeah, sure. She's right here. We're getting ready to film. Do you want me to ask her for you?"

Cassie shot him a quizzical look and mouthed, *What?*

Logan smiled and held up a finger.

"That would be great," Bunny said. "I was going to call her next. But since she's right there, you go ahead and extend the invitation for me. Tell her I'm making my famous lasagna."

"I will. I'm sure she won't want to miss out on that. What time?"

"Six o'clock for cocktails. Dinner at seven sharp."

After he hung up the phone, Cassie asked, "What don't I want to miss out on?"

"That was my mother. I hope you don't have plans for tonight, because you have officially been summoned to a McFadden family dinner."

Cassie reminded herself that she had no reason to be anxious—it was just a dinner with her cast mates—but that didn't override the nerves.

She inhaled through her nose for four counts, held it for seven counts and then exhaled for eight, practicing the rhythmic breathing technique her yoga teacher back in Florida had prescribed to help her with the anxiety she'd experienced after she'd learned about Troy and Marissa.

This was not anything like when she'd gone to Troy's house for dinner for the first time. This wasn't even in the same arena. The McFaddens were such nice people …and they were her colleagues. Cassie was making her own way in the world. She wasn't the criminal's daughter that the Houston family had tolerated. She and Troy had been in high school when she first met his family. They were just kids, but that hadn't made his mom, Mary Jane Houston, any warmer to her.

She blinked away the thought. Troy, Marissa and Mary Jane Houston were not invited tonight, and she would not let them tag along in spirit.

There's nothing to be nervous about tonight. In fact, it's nice that they invited you over to the family dinner.

Or better yet, she could think of it as a business dinner or a dinner party with friends, she coached herself as the car's GPS instructed her to turn in to the next driveway on the left. She did, but that was as far as she could go. A closed wrought iron gate blocked her way. She rolled down the window and pressed the button on the call box that was situated on a post alongside the cobblestone driveway.

"May I help you?" asked a disembodied voice.

"Hello, Cassie Houston here to see Mr. and Mrs. McFadden."

There was a pause, and then the voice said, "Welcome, Cassie. It's Bert. Please come in."

As if by magic, the gate slid open, and she drove through.

If she hadn't been nervous before, she was now.

Neat rows of Italian cypress trees lined each side of the driveway, giving an added air of seclusion and privacy. A few feet ahead, she spied an ornate lighted fountain in the center of the circular driveway in front of a sprawling Mediterranean mansion.

In addition to Logan's black truck, four more cars and the Top Drawer Productions vans were parked in the driveway.

As she parked next to Logan, she glanced at the

dashboard clock. Based on the time that Logan had given her, she was a few minutes early.

But holy cow. This house.

It was huge. It made Troy's family home, which Cassie had found intimidating the first time she'd visited, look downright ordinary.

Cassie swallowed the nerves that threatened to coil around her airways, making it difficult to breathe, and gave herself a pep talk.

Being nervous was ridiculous, because the Mc-Faddens were so down-to-earth. And Logan, in his blue jeans and black truck, had seemed so...un-ho-ity-toity...was that even a word?

Bottom line was she hadn't expected the house to be so grand, but why wouldn't it be, since the entire family was in luxury real estate?

She hoped the production team was just here for dinner and they weren't planning on filming tonight. However, a couple of crew members were unloading equipment and coiling cords around their arms, which made the outlook for a quiet dinner unpromising.

She was exhausted. After they'd filmed at Broadhurst House, Logan had driven her back to Baxter and Mason, where she'd placed the order for delivery tomorrow. Then he drove her back to the office so she could pick up her car. She'd barely had time to get home, tend to Luna, shower and get ready before heading back out. The upside was when she'd gotten home, the AC in her house was working and had cooled down the place, which meant she had been able to get ready in a blessedly cool house, and she hadn't perspired off her makeup before she'd gotten dressed. She took it as a sign that it would be a good night.

She checked her makeup in the rearview mirror one last time, then gathered the bouquet of flowers that she had brought for Bunny, suddenly second-guessing whether or not they were appropriate now that she'd gotten a glimpse of the fabulous McFadden abode.

Her mother had always told her not to show up to a dinner party empty-handed. Since she was short on time and she didn't know the good places to go, she had decided that flowers were a better choice than a grocery store candle or wine that was within her budget.

It was the thought that counted, wasn't it?

She hoped so as she let herself out of the car and took another deep breath. The smell of the sea air wafted in on the gentle evening breeze. It offered a break from the oppressive humidity that had dominated the day and calmed her nerves.

As she walked on the balls of her feet to keep her heels from getting caught between the cobblestones, she heard a car door open.

Logan unfolded himself from his truck and smiled at her.

"Fancy seeing you here," she said.

"I've been here a time or two." His voice was deep, and it sent a frisson of awareness swirling through her. "Are those flowers for me?"

"Sorry, they're for Bunny," she said. "Why were you sitting in your truck? Are you hiding from the film crew?"

"How'd you know?" He smiled, and there was that dimple winking at her, setting her at ease.

"I didn't realize it would be a working dinner," she said, glad she'd dressed up.

"Who knows?" he said. "I wasn't exactly avoiding them. I needed to make some calls before I went inside. My mother has a strict no-cell-phone policy when the family gets together."

"That's probably a good rule," Cassie said. "I can imagine the phone calls and texts might take away from family time."

"You barely know my mother and you're already taking her side," he said. "Are you trying to score points?"

Cassie raised her brows, doing her best not to show that she was wondering what he meant by *scoring points*. If they were dating, she could understand it, but… "I know Bunny well enough to understand that she is a wise woman. I happen to agree with her no-cell-phone policy. If good manners mean scoring points, so be it."

"I was talking about the flowers." He nodded to

the bouquet. "Peonies are her favorite flower. Well done."

"I guess your mom and I have that in common, too," she said. "As far as I'm concerned, anyone who invites me for homemade lasagna deserves bushels of peonies, but this was the last bouquet the florist had in stock. So, this meager offering will have to suffice."

Logan put his hand on the small of Cassie's back as they stepped onto the front porch. Awareness zinged through her, and she hoped her sharp intake of breath wasn't obvious. He opened the front door and motioned for Cassie to enter ahead of him.

Once inside, Cassie glanced around the foyer. A gold and white Murano glass chandelier hung in the entryway. It was reflected in a large gilt-framed mirror that hung above an exquisite mahogany console table that boasted ornate golden rams' heads at the top of each of the cabriole legs and tapered off to slender golden hooves at the base.

A large vase of white flowers that looked as if they belonged in the lobby of a five-star hotel adorned the center of the table.

She could hear voices sounding from the other room.

Logan extended a hand and gestured for Cassie to enter the room first.

"Hi, Mom." Logan said from behind her.

Bunny stood from her place on the sofa. "Hello,

sweetheart." Logan bent and kissed her on the cheek. "I'm so happy you're here.

"Hello, Cassie. Welcome." She smiled and took Cassie's hand in hers. She looked as if she spent her days at the country club on the tennis courts rather than working all day in a hot kitchen making home-made lasagna. "It's good to see you again. Did the two of you come here together?"

There was a warm, almost mischievous sparkle in Bunny's eyes that instantly put Cassie at ease. Cassie was struck with how Bunny and Bert McFadden seemed to be polar opposites. Maybe the McFadden men got the quiet gene and the women were more gregarious.

"No, Mom," Logan said. "We just happened to arrive at the same time."

"These are for you, Bunny." Cassie held out the flowers, and Bunny took them and buried her nose in the blossoms.

"Aren't you the sweetest thing." she said. "They are just beautiful. If y'all will excuse me, I'll put them in water. Logan, would you please get yourself and Cassie something to drink?"

After Bunny returned with the peonies in a beautiful crystal vase, she set them in the middle of the coffee table and Dalton called everyone to order by pinging his glass with a flick of his thumb and index finger.

"Hello, everyone," he said. "First, I'd like to thank

Bunny and Bert for having everyone over for dinner tonight, and I'd like to propose a toast to a successful start to filming *Selling Sandcastle*."

He raised his rocks glass, which held about three fingers' worth of bourbon, and everyone followed suit with a chorus of "cheers!"

"Don't kill me, but we're not done yet," he continued. "We want to get some footage of tonight's dinner."

When he was met with silence, he said, "Since the crew is setting up, I'm sure that doesn't come as a surprise. And since you're being such team players, I have a surprise for you. Each of you gets to plan two scenes that show you as you want the TV world to see you. You get to choose who you will film with, even if it's someone who isn't a cast member."

He motioned to his assistant Kara, and she passed out papers with the details. On the back was a form with space for them to write down the names of the people with whom they wanted to shoot, the location of the shoot and basic details of what the scene would be about. This started a chorus of murmurs and questions.

"You don't need to tell me right away," he said. "Think about it and get your forms back to Kara or Zoe by Friday?"

Immediately, Sophie came over to Cassie and said, "Let's film together."

"You read my mind," Cassie said. "I was also

thinking about having my sister, Gabby, come up to film. She'd kill me if I didn't include her. Especially since she's largely responsible for me being here."

Cassie told Sophie about Gabby dragging her to the open audition for the cooking competition and how that led to Dalton contacting her for *Selling Sandcastle*.

By the time she'd finished, she realized that Logan had moved closer and was listening to her talk. She made a mental note to ask him if they could do a scene together. Her stomach fluttered at the thought. She felt like a kid back in high school contemplating asking a guy to the Sadie Hawkins dance. But this was all business. The on-camera storyline had him showing her the ropes. Doing yet another scene together seemed only natural.

"Yes, we have to include Gabby," Sophie said. "We can plan the shoot to be a girls' night out."

"I like what I'm hearing," Dalton said.

He motioned for the camera operator to come over.

"This would be a good place to start filming tonight," he said. "Sophie, can you and Cassie recreate what you were just talking about, but in more general terms? Leave out the part about the filming the future scenes and the audition, of course, because that kills the fantasy element. Reframe it to talk about what brought Cassie to Tinsley Cove and about having her sister come up for some girl time. Bunny, come over here, too, and join in. And Logan—you step into frame after we start rolling. You're going to bring Cassie a glass of wine." Dalton plucked Cassie's glass out of her hand, and a production assistant whisked it away.

Cassie's heart beat wildly and leaped at the thought of Logan being part of this supposedly non-work-related scene.

As soon as the lights were in place and the camera was rolling, she was surprised by how natural it felt to talk to Sophie and Bunny. They were so warm and welcoming. They made her feel like one of them as they talked about how happy they were to have her as part of the Sandcastle team. Sophie backtracked to their earlier conversation about having Gabby come up from Orlando for a girls' night.

When Logan handed her the glass of wine and slid into the conversation, it felt seamless and natural and kind of fun. Until Bunny innocently said, "I was so sorry to hear that both of your folks have passed on, Cassie. That must've been so difficult for you and your sister, but I'll bet it's made you even closer."

Cassie froze.

Whoa. Wait a minute. Rewind.

Technically, she'd never said *both* of her parents were *dead*. She'd said they were *gone*. While "dead" meant *dead*, "gone" could mean *away*. She'd said it off camera, in a place where she believed it wouldn't be broadcast to the world.

However, now she knew anything that was said to the cast or crew was fodder for when they were filming. How could she not have realized that during that first show-and-tell session?

Bunny hadn't meant any harm. Of course not. She was only going by what Cassie had told her.

For a split second, Cassie considered setting the record straight. Then she glanced at Logan, who standing next to her, watching her intently, waiting for her answer.

In that instant, she decided telling the world that her father was in prison and had been there since she was six years old was just too messy. After she'd told Troy's parents the truth about her dad's past, they'd never looked at her the same way.

People loved to charge the child for the sins of the father. There was no way she was going to put herself on trial in the court of public opinion.

"Yes, Gabby and I are very close. She's the best sister. Bunny, your lasagna smells amazing. I can't wait to try it."

Chapter Nine

The day of Picnic in the Park in downtown Tinsley Cove dawned sunny and warm. It was the perfect day for filming, and Logan was scheduled to work the hot dog and snow cone booth that Forest had sponsored to support his mayoral campaign.

When Logan opened his eyes that morning, he realized he wasn't even dreading it. Maybe it was because they'd been filming for about two weeks now and it was starting to become a way of life. Maybe even a habit to live his life with a camera following him.

Maybe not a habit, because he'd heard somewhere that it took three weeks for something like that to stick. Maybe he wasn't dreading it because he and Cassie were scheduled to work the same shift.

As much as he'd resented being on this show in the beginning, he had to admit it was an interesting diversion from his life in California. Until he'd come home, he hadn't even realized how solitary his day-to-day existence had become. Getting up every day, working construction jobs and coming home only to do it all over again the next day.

He had no money and too much debt to waste what he did earn on going out drinking with the other guys on the crew after work. It had earned him a reputation of being aloof and unsociable, but he didn't care. People who worked construction could be transient. So what was the point of getting to know anyone? Even when it came to the handful who showed up day after day, like he did, they didn't want to hear his sob story about losing his wife and gaining a mountain of debt as a consolation prize.

He'd managed to lie low since he'd been home, filming with family members and Cassie at various homes they'd listed, but today would be a bit more public focused. Not only were they filming in the middle of downtown Tinsley Cove, but now that the production was in a groove, they were making the official announcement about the show to the locals. That meant it was more likely that he would run into people he hadn't seen in years. Some would know about Natalie. Others were bound to ask after her.

He felt his mood slipping into dark territory.

Cassie would be there. Not that he intended to

hide behind her—because that was sure to start
tongues wagging. Another thing he'd learned over
the past two weeks—when he thought the worst was
going to happen, she somehow managed to make it
not so bad.

So Logan turned on the shower as hot as he could
stand it and washed away the dark thoughts.

The house he was renting from Sandcastle Real
Estate was located downtown. So he downed a bowl
of cereal and a cup of coffee and set off on foot for
the festival in Springdale Park.

Even before he passed a group of food trucks in
the lot next to the park, he could hear one of the local
bands that had been hired to play the festival. They
were up on the covered stage at one end of the park.
People sat on lawn chairs and on blankets eating picnic lunches and listening to them play. A handful of
people stood next to the stage dancing to the music.

As Logan wound his way through the maze of
booths that were set up on the grass, selling refresh-
ments like lemonade and ice cream and fun like bal-
loons, temporary tattoos and face painting, he finally
located the Forest McFadden for Mayor booth.

He was surprised by the crowd gathered around
the booth. While his dad and Owen gave away hot
dogs and snow cones hand over fist, Forest stood in
front of the booth holding court with his potential
constituents, who seemed genuinely interested in
what he had to say.

Then Logan saw Cassie standing over to the side of the booth, and the mere sight of her made something inside him finally feel like he was home. She looked gorgeous in the green-and-blue dress she was wearing. It showed off those long, tanned legs. Logan had to force himself not to let his gaze meander over the length of her body. It was easier said than done. Instead, he focused on her corgi.

Cassie had brought Luna with her. While she was pouring water from a bottle into the dog's bowl, Sophie and his mom were tying a McFadden for Mayor bandanna around Luna's neck and straightening out the back cape-style so that people could see the campaign message.

"Forget the hot dogs," Sophie cooed as she scratched under the dog's chin. "This little girl is drawing people in. She's your perfect mascot, Forest."

It was true—a small crowd had gathered around. People were oohing and ahhing over the good-natured pup, who was lapping up the attention like kibbles and bits raining down from the heavens.

When Cassie turned around and saw Logan, her face lit up. She waved at him and made her way over to stand next to him. "There's my booth buddy."

Buddy? His mind automatically equated *buddy* with being relegated to the friend zone. He had to sort that out, because they *were* friends. Nothing more. And they were working the next shift at Forest's booth together. Though it appeared that his brother had plenty of help, since his entire family seemed content to be hanging out.

"Do they need all of us?" he asked. "I don't know that there's enough room for all of us to get behind the booth."

Cassie glanced at her watch. "It's about five minutes before our shift officially starts. That's why your dad and Owen are still working, but I'm sure they'd be happy if we wanted to relieve them. They've been hopping since I've been here. Your mom and Sophie offered to tend to Luna while you and I are tending the booth. It's a good thing, too. I wouldn't have brought her if I'd known it was going to be this busy. But it's good, because Forest is really working this crowd. I think he has a good chance of being elected."

The thing about Cassie was she always seemed to see the good in everything. One person could view today as a chore—being stuck tending a campaign booth on a hot and sticky Saturday morning—but judging by the smile on her face, there was no doubt that she saw it as spending the day at a fun community festival.

There it was again—she'd made him see that the glass could just as easily be half-full rather than half-empty.

The band started playing a song about being

happy together, and she danced to the beat and started singing along under her breath.

The sight of her carefree, go-with-the-flow way made him smile.

"What?" she asked.

"I don't know," he said. "I guess I'm just taking it all in."

She put her hand on his arm and leaned in so she could talk over the music. "Oh, I forgot to tell you. Dalton was here just before you arrived, and he said that he's going to have us all go up on stage after our shift ends so he can announce that we're filming *Selling Sandcastle*."

Logan had known that there was a good possibility that Dalton would make the announcement today. He hadn't realized they'd all have to go up onstage. Dalton was a hometown guy, too. For some reason, Logan had gotten it in his head that since Dalton was the producer and director of the show that he would want the total spotlight.

Going up onstage was different than filming on a closed set. Getting up there in front of all those people felt like being exposed in the worst way.

"Does he need all of us up there?" Logan asked.

Cassie nodded. "It sounded more like a summons rather than an invitation."

With the exception of running into Natalie's friend Lindy Hendrickson, he'd managed to lie low for two weeks. He shouldn't be surprised that refuge was coming to an end.

Just as Cassie had said it would happen, an hour later, after their shift, Dalton appeared at the booth and shepherded the entire cast toward the stage, including Lucy, who had shown up after a prior obligation with a college class she was taking.

Though they were out of hot dogs and snow cones, Kara and Zoe looked after Luna and occupied the Forest McFadden for Mayor booth, passing out campaign information to some and directing others to the stage to hear an *exciting announcement*.

Sheila Larson, the president of the chamber of commerce, introduced Dalton, praising him as Tinsley Cove's own hometown superstar, which seemed a little overblown, but after all, this business was all about the hype.

Dalton got up onstage and made the big announcement. Cassie and Logan waited behind the stage with the rest of his family. They stood so close that their upper arms were pressed against each other. Rather than pulling away to reclaim his personal space, Logan stayed next to her, soaking up the comfort and…what was that extra feeling?

"I am beyond thrilled to be home," Dalton called over cheers from the audience. "You know what makes me even happier? I'm ecstatic that I can feature my beloved hometown in a show that will be featured on the Home, Hearth and Garden Network beginning this fall."

A female voice from the audience called, "I love you, Dalton."

"Well, thank you, whoever you are. I'm sure I love you, too," Dalton said back.

As the crowd cracked up, Logan looked down at Cassie, and their gazes snared and held. The way she smiled at him made him realize that, for the first time in a long time, he could feel something other than shame, pain, and self-loathing.

He felt alive.

He reached down and took her hand in his as they listened to Dalton continue with the introduction.

"We all know what a cool place Tinsley Cove is. *Huh? Huh?* Am I right?"

The crowd cheered.

"I'm confident that the television show *Selling Sandcastle*, featuring our very own beloved Mc-Fadden family and their costar Cassie Houston, will show the rest of the world what we already know."

As Logan and Cassie smiled at each other and allowed themselves to get jazzed by Dalton's hype, a woman stopped next to Logan.

"Logan? Honey, is that you?"

Logan stiffened when he turned and saw Lorraine and Bob Holmes, Natalie's parents, whom he hadn't seen since his late wife's funeral, standing there like they'd seen a ghost.

* * *

It had been a deflating letdown, Cassie groused as she opened the car door and helped Luna out of her safety harness and down from the back seat.

One minute Logan had been holding her hand right there in front of God and his whole family. It felt as if they were caught in some sort of magnetic tractor beam, hypnotizing them, shutting out the world except for the two of them.

Then the older couple had appeared, and Logan had flinched away from Cassie like she'd burned him. Logan had stayed behind to talk to the man and woman even after Dalton had called them up onstage. Then, after the announcement was finished, Logan had disappeared. He'd been nowhere to be found.

That's when Sophie told her that the couple were his former in-laws.

"I'm sure it was awkward, since he hasn't seen them since the funeral," Sophie said as she and Cassie walked to the car. Since they lived next door to each other, Cassie had offered to drive. "I kept telling him he needed to go over and see them and tell them he was back in town before he ran into them. But that brother of mine is so hardheaded he won't listen. I know it was hard for him. And I'm sure they were all surprised by the encounter, but it's his own fault."

Cassie tried to keep her face neutral as Sophie

filled her in. Even more important, she forced herself not to interject, because if she was talking, Sophie wouldn't be filling her in.

But Cassie couldn't help but feel strange that Sophie hadn't mentioned anything about the way Logan had been holding Cassie's hand and that there had clearly been vibes zinging back and forth between them.

She sighed inwardly. Maybe she was reading more into this than was really there. After all, Dalton had told them to play up the chemistry. Maybe she had mistaken him playing a part for genuine interest.

"I know he still blames himself for Natalie's death," Sophie said. "I just wish he could talk to Mr. and Mrs. Holmes and see that they don't in any way hold him responsible."

Cassie was so tempted to ask Sophie what had happened that would make Logan hold himself responsible, but it felt like she would be prying. That information needed to come from Logan.

Instead, she changed the subject. "Dalton didn't seem very happy about Logan skipping out on the media introduction. I hope Logan will talk to him so that things don't get tense."

The truth was Cassie hoped that just maybe Sophie would tell her a little more, but the ever-faithful sister shook her head as she hitched her purse up onto her shoulder and said, "Sometimes Logan can be so hardheaded. Frankly, I hope Dalton doesn't fire his ass for what he did. It would serve Logan right. But this show is important to our mom, and even more, it's important to her that we're all on the show. So, I think once Logan figures out he's goofed in a big way, he'll find a way to make it right. I need to run. I'm showing a rental at five."

After that, Cassie prepared herself to spend a quiet Saturday night at home. It wasn't such a bad thing. She could use the time to finish unpacking.

She took a shower to wash off the day's heat and humidity and had just changed into shorts and a T-shirt and was contemplating what she would order in for dinner when her phone pinged.

Logan: Are you busy?

Her heart lurched into her throat.

She typed, I'm always busy. But then deleted it, because ugh. No. That didn't come across the way she thought it would—light and a little funny, with the subtext that she wasn't just sitting around waiting for him to come over and hold her hand again.

She typed, Why? What's going on?

Logan: Wanted to talk to you. May I come over?

The butterflies fluttered to life. She thought about asking him if he'd talked to Dalton and if not shouldn't he do that first…but *nah*, of course he could come over.

She typed, Sure. Give me thirty minutes.

Mentally high-fiving herself for taking a shower first thing, she raced to dry her hair and put on a little makeup—CC cream, bronzer, mascara and natural lip color—just enough to look like she hadn't tried as hard as she was trying to look effortlessly polished. She pulled on a pair of jeans and a gauzy black-and-white off-the-shoulder blouse. It wasn't exactly an outfit that she'd wear to hang around the house, but Logan didn't know that.

She had just enough time to toss on a cuff bracelet before he knocked on the door, sending Luna into a tailspin and making Cassie's heart pound overtime. She took a calming deep breath—in for four counts, hold for seven counts, out for eight counts. Then he knocked again.

It wouldn't hurt to make him wait a minute.

Then she remembered the dreaded doorbell camera. There was no doubt that nosy Dalton and company would be all over this. As she walked to the door, she wondered if she would've been so eager to sign up if she'd known that they'd be watching her comings and goings.

Yeah, she still probably would've done it.

"Luna, *shhhhhh*!" Cassie hissed. "I'm sure you know who that is on the other side of the door, but you need to chill."

She opened the door, and Luna lunged at Logan, delivering dozens of kisses. He caught her and herded the little dog back inside.

Cassie took care to stay back far enough so that she wouldn't be within the doorbell camera's range. She closed the door behind Logan.

"Doorbell cam," she said.

He groaned and scowled.

"I know you're not my landlord, but maybe you can tell me why I'm the one who lives here, but Dalton gets to be the keeper of the doorbell-cam footage. Aren't those things meant to protect the occupant of the house by letting them see who's outside their door rather than allowing someone else to monitor the comings and goings of the resident?"

Logan stared at her for a couple of beats, as if he was actually giving it some thought.

"Good question," he said. "You might want to ask Sophie. It probably has something to do with the production company paying for the lease, but I think you view the footage on doorbell cams through an app on your phone. Maybe they can hook you up, too?"

Cassie shrugged. "It's worth checking. Although, even if I have access, Dalton probably still would, too. I guess we just need to watch what we're doing as we come and go."

"You look nice," he said.

Her heart kicked into high gear again as she remembered he hadn't come over to discuss doorbell cameras.

"Thank you. So, where did you go today?"

She figured she might as well jump right to the point.

Logan sat on the couch, resting his right ankle on his left knee and leaning down to scratch Luna behind the ear where she was sitting leaning against his left leg.

"That's what I came to talk to you about," he finally said, staring down at the dog as seconds of silence ticked away.

It was one of the most difficult things she'd ever done, but she forced herself to stay silent until he spoke again.

"The man and woman who approached me right before we went onstage are my—err—Natalie's parents." He sat back and crossed his arms over his chest. "The sad thing is, I don't even know what to call them anymore—my in-laws? But I'm not married to their daughter anymore. My ex-in-laws? It's not like Natalie and I broke up—"

He grimaced. "Sorry, I didn't mean that like it was a…"

"No problem. That's what I was talking about earlier this week. Troy and I had a choice to stay together or not. You and Natalie didn't. But this isn't about Troy and me. Are you still close to them? If you are and you're worried that they might get offended since they saw you holding my hand, I can—"

"No. That's not it at all."

Okay, then, what is it?

He held up his hands, then raked them through his hair, exhaling a heavy sigh.

"The thing is, we used to be close, but I haven't seen or talked to them since Natalie's funeral."

"Communication is a two-way street. You can't just blame yourself."

"Yes, I can. They tried to stay in touch. They called and emailed, but I couldn't bring myself to answer any of it. I know, that's pretty crappy." He took another deep breath and seemed to be weighing his words. "So when I saw them today, it was kind of hard on a couple of different levels. We were just getting ready to go onstage, but I couldn't just say, *Oh, hey,* and turn around and walk away. So we went to the Bean and Press coffee shop and had a cup of coffee and a good long talk."

"How did it go? I mean, I'm guessing you don't mind me asking or you wouldn't have brought it up."

"I don't mind. In fact, that's why I came over. They were…they are the best people. I told them that I hadn't been able to keep in touch because I blamed myself for what happened to Natalie."

"What did they say?"

Logan shrugged. "They insist it's not my fault. Despite the…"

He shook his head as if he was clearing it of all thoughts of Natalie.

"Logan, do you mind if I ask what happened?" Cassie held her breath, afraid he might tell her it was none of her business and get up and walk out.

He stared past her into the middle distance for a moment. Cassie lowered herself onto the chair across from him and bit down on her bottom lip until Logan started speaking again.

"Natalie loved pretty things, and she loved to shop. Of course, I didn't want to deny her anything, but I was trying to get my business off the ground, and she had this dream of being a social media content creator—or, what do they call it? An influencer? Whatever it is, it doesn't bring in any cash until you make a name for yourself. Long story short, she ended up racking up a lot of debt. But she came to me about it, saying she had to make herself look like an influencer before she could gain enough followers to interest companies to start paying her to rep their products. You know, fake it until you make it.

"We agreed that we couldn't afford that kind of lifestyle, but we figured out how to pay off that debt, and she promised me she'd never do it again. She swore she'd be up-front about the things she bought. I believed her. We all make mistakes." He closed his eyes for a moment and shook his head.

"Well, about a year and a half later, a collections agency called, and I found out that she'd racked up more than a hundred thousand dollars in debt. She'd lied to me and told me all the clothes and beauty products and trips she'd taken for location shoots were paid for by sponsors. She made it seem as if she was finally living her dream. I didn't know any different—that's not my thing. I don't do social media. But she was smart and beautiful, and I believed anyone would be lucky to have her repping their brands. In reality what was happening was she was shifting the credit card debt she'd accrued from one card to another. Finally, she'd reached the end of the line—she couldn't make her payments and she couldn't get any more credit.

"I flipped out."

Cassie shrank away and crossed her arms, afraid of what he would say next. He must've read it on her face.

"No, it's not what you're thinking. I was never violent. I never raised a hand to her…but it's still bad."

He put both feet on the floor and leaned forward with his forearms on his knees. He stared at the floor.

"When I confronted her, she got defensive. At first, she tried to deny it. Then I told her the collection agency was trying to collect the debt from me."

"Wait a minute," Cassie said. "Unless you co-signed for the credit card or it was a joint account, they can't hold you liable, can they?"

"California is a community property state. Since

the debt was incurred while we were married, I'm responsible for it."

"Oh, jeez," Cassie whispered.

Logan nodded. "I was furious, and not just because of the mountain of debt. I was really done in by her lies. She *lied* to me. She knew how hard it was to pay off the debt the first time. She promised—" His voice caught on the last word, and when he lifted his head, Cassie saw that he had tears in his eyes.

He cleared his throat. "She promised it wouldn't happen again, and then she racks up four times the original amount, and she lied to me about it. She lied about not doing it again. She lied about where all the fancy dresses and expensive products were from. Then, when I confronted her, she stood there and looked me in the face and denied it all. Until she realized that the collection agency was coming after me."

Cassie swallowed hard. "Oh my gosh." She had a sick feeling she knew where this story was going and how it was going to end. She sat there in silence with Logan until he was ready to continue.

"Finally she admitted it was true," he said. "She said she loved me and she promised she'd find a way to fix it. She'd get a job with a steady paycheck and pay off every cent herself." He shook his head. "I was so furious. All I could say was 'You lied to me. When are you going to learn you can't fix things with an apology and a pretty smile?' She got upset and grabbed her keys and her purse and said, 'Fine. Be mad. Let me know when you want to talk about it.' Those were the last words we said to each other. She jumped into her car and cranked up the radio. That damn Rascal Flatts song was playing, and she sat there for a few seconds looking at me. I just stood there like an idiot and watched her throw the car in Reverse and back out of the driveway. She was looking at me, not where she was going. A car hit her broadside."

Cassie gasped, and her hand fluttered to her neck. "Was she killed instantly?"

"Nope. She was on life support for more than a week until they finally pronounced her brain-dead. If I had just gone to the car and made her get out—"

A single sob escaped Logan's throat, and Cassie got up from the chair and sat down next to him on the couch. She put her arms around him, and they held each other.

Time seemed to stand still, and the rest of the world slipped away. Cassie wasn't sure how long they sat that way. All she knew was that he smelled of cedar cologne and laundry detergent. If not that he was crying on her shoulder over his late wife, she could stay like this forever, happily breathing him in.

Finally he pulled away.

"I'm sorry. I didn't mean to dump all of this on you."

It was a lot, but she was glad he'd confided in her.

"I almost hate to even bring this up, but you started to tell me how things went with your in-laws—and, by the way, if you still love them and they're good people, there's no reason you can't still call them your in-laws. They're still in your life. But that's just my opinion, and I'll be quiet now so you can tell me the rest."

He smiled and actually chuckled a bit. "Yes, they're great people. That's another facet of why this hurts so much. I took their daughter away from them and—"

Cassie held up her hand. "Hold on there. I'm going to assume that when you say you took their daughter away from them you mean you took her across the country, because Natalie's death is not your fault, Logan. You have to stop blaming yourself. She was responsible for her own actions. I know I haven't known you very long, but I'm pretty sure you're not *that* controlling that you think you could've stopped her."

"Yeah, but—"

"But nothing," Cassie said. "It's tragic. It stinks. It's so unfair my heart is broken for you, but it's also unfair for you to keep blaming and punishing yourself for something you didn't do."

He opened his mouth like he was going to say something but closed it again. He raked both hands into his hair and held them on his head as if he was holding himself together. Cassie hoped that maybe the realization that he actually wasn't to blame for Natalie's death was so mind-blowing he felt like he had to hold his head together.

Finally, he slumped forward again, resting his elbows on his knees and putting his face in his hands. When he looked up at her again, he said, "That's exactly what Lorraine and Bob Holmes said to me this afternoon. They don't blame me, and they want me to stop blaming myself and get on with my life."

Cassie reached out and put her hand on his shoulder. "So what are you waiting for?"

Then her stomach growled so loudly it made Luna bark and them laugh. There was a seismic shift in the mood.

They decided to order in Thai food. He got pad Thai, and she ordered the massaman curry. They ate together, sharing bites of their dishes.

Cassie could feel that something had shifted between them, but it still felt fragile. Plus, she had vowed that these weeks in Tinsley Cove were time for her. Time to figure out what she wanted without tying herself to someone else who was still healing himself. Maybe she was getting ahead of herself, as she had a track record of doing.

For now she could use a friend…a breathtakingly sexy friend who smelled good and whose arms felt like a healing sanctuary…even though she was the one who had been comforting him.

Yes, for now, they were in a good place, and there wasn't a thing wrong with it.

After they'd cleaned up the dinner plates and conversation became quiet, Logan said, "Well, I'd better go."

He stood by the front door with his hand on the knob, but he didn't seem in a big hurry to leave.

"I meant to ask you." Cassie grimaced. "Have you talked to Dalton about why you didn't go onstage?"

Logan nodded. "I called him after I left Lorraine and Bob. Dalton was surprisingly cool about it."

"Good, because on another day the Dalton we know and love could've been decidedly unhinged over it."

They laughed, and then they were quiet and Logan was looking at her in a way that made her stomach ripple.

Was he going to kiss her?

She wouldn't mind if he did and even considered leaning in and making the first move.

Then he shifted his gaze to his hand on the doorknob, and the moment had passed. She was inexplicably disappointed, even though she knew tonight wasn't the night for something like that…not after the emotional outpouring over Natalie.

As he twisted the knob, she cried, "Wait! Don't go out there."

He held his hands up in surrender. "Um, okay. Why? My truck is out there."

"So is the doorbell cam," she whispered. "Let's mess with Dalton's mind. He saw you come in, and you know he's going to watch to see what time you leave. He would be so baffled if he never saw you leave."

"He might think I spent the night."

The thought of Logan spending the night—naked in her queen-size bed…their limbs tangled, like their fingers had been entwined, only better…so much better… *Stop!*

"No, he won't. He'll see me leave solo in the morning, and you'll be a mystery."

Actually, Dalton would think that for the rest of the evening. They would get his hopes up that his chemistry experiment had finally built up to a combustible point, only to crush them when she finally emerged alone.

"Ahh, I get it." Logan hooked a thumb in the direction of the back door.

Cassie nodded. The doorbell cam only covered the porch. It didn't reach all the way over to the driveway.

The two of them went out the back door into the inky night. Logan laughed. "I wish I could be a fly on the wall as Dalton's imagination starts running wild."

Cassie laughed, too. "Can you even imagine?"

They walked to his truck, and she followed him around to the driver's side, casting a glance in the direction of the front porch to make sure they were out of camera range.

From where they stood, she couldn't see the camera. So it stood to reason if she couldn't see it, it couldn't see them.

They should be safe.

Logan opened the truck door but didn't immediately climb into the cab. He stood there with his right hand on the top of the door frame, looking like he wanted to say something.

It took every fiber of discipline in her being not to fill the silence. Instead, she stood there, waiting for him to go first, ignoring the inane voice in her head that asked, *What if he's thinking about kissing you now?*

Finally, he said, "Thanks, Cassie."

It felt like a letdown, like a handshake between acquaintances.

She waited for him to say more, but he didn't. As he started to climb into the truck, she said, "Wait, Logan."

He turned around to face her.

"When I look at you, I see a guy who is caring and loyal and would never purposely hurt somebody he loved. I know you've been through hell and back, but you can't keep torturing yourself. You have to give yourself some grace. Will you please do that?"

They stood there for a moment, him looking as if he was processing what she'd asked. Then he made a gesture that was half nod, half shrug.

"At least try to be kind to yourself. Okay?" She

leaned in to give him a one-armed hug. She'd intended for it to be a quick, friendly good-night squeeze between friends, but when he didn't pull away, she didn't, either.

He held her, tentatively, as if giving her a chance to let go, to step back and reclaim her space. Instead, she slid her other arm around him, buried her face in his shoulder and breathed in the fresh cedar-and-laundry scent of him. He pulled her closer and nuzzled his face into her hair. She could feel his breath hot on her temple.

If she turned her head just the slightest bit to the right, their lips would be so close.

So. Close.

Then Sophie's voice cut through the darkness. "Logan? Is that you? Is everything okay?"

Chapter Ten

Cassie spent a restless night dreaming about how it felt to be in Logan's arms. Would he have kissed her if Sophie hadn't interrupted them?

Did she want to kiss him?

Of course she did. Or at least that's what her subconscious told her as she'd tossed and turned in that hazy limbo between dreaming and wakefulness.

However, right now she was fully awake and she knew that Sophie's interruption had been a blessing in disguise.

Muddying the waters with a kiss, which would've only made them crave more, was the last thing either of them needed. It was better to build a solid friendship, a strong working relationship, and not mess up the good opportunity they had with *Selling Sandcastle* with romance.

Of course, if it came down to it, Logan would stay since he was part of the McFadden family. She would go since she was the outsider.

Plus, she rationalized, right now, they were both confused. It was as if they were both coming up for air after being underground for an extended period of time. They were blinking at the sunlight, unsure which direction to go. Two lost souls trying to find their way. Invariably, they would find that, in the end, they were headed in two vastly different directions.

Thank goodness today was Sunday, a day off. She would finish unpacking—exactly what she had planned to do last night before Logan showed up. But that was all right. Even though he didn't owe her an explanation, he had come over yesterday to fill her in on what had happened with Natalie's parents rather than waiting until Monday, when they were scheduled to film together.

After eating a bowl of oatmeal and brewing herself a second cup of coffee, Cassie set to work unpacking the last of the remaining boxes. Of course, they were all clothes. She should've asked Gabby to store some of her things, because she'd never wear most of them. It wasn't like she was moving to the frozen tundra where she could wear sweaters and jackets. But there was something decidedly comforting about having her pretty things all around her.

They were like old friends. Friends she could count on—not like Marissa, who'd used her to get close to Troy, taken what she wanted and then kicked Cassie to the curb.

Because her mom was sick when she was in high school, she'd devoted so much time to taking care of her, taking her to doctors' appointments and bringing her cold compresses for her head and fixing her ginger tea to help soothe her stomach after the chemo ravaged her system, she hadn't had time for girlfriends.

Her mom, Gabby and Troy had been her whole life. Cassie believed if she took good enough care of her mom, she would kick cancer's butt and get back to being the superwoman she had always been the entire time she had raised Gabby and Cassie as a single parent.

Her mother had died when Cassie was eighteen and Gabby was nineteen. It dawned on Cassie that maybe a person was only given so much life to spend—like currency—and by the time Ona May Davis had succumbed to the cancer that had ravaged her body, eating her up and spitting out her tiny eighty-eight-pound frame, her account was surely overdrawn.

Cassie and Gabby had consoled themselves by marveling over how the three of them had loved so much and so well in spite of all the hardship. In the comparatively short amount of time they'd had together on this earth, they had loved more than some people loved in a lifetime.

Troy had stood by her side, propping her up and promising her he would make everything okay. Proving that, he'd proposed to Cassie six weeks after she had buried her mother. His parents had pitched a fit. They said he was too young. He had been tied down to Cassie since they were fourteen. He was just starting college. He needed to get out and live a little before settling down.

Cassie read between the lines and knew the subtext was that they didn't want their beloved baby boy tethered to the daughter of a con man who was serving hard time.

Cassie had learned her lesson about telling people about the father she didn't even know. Rather than telling people the truth—that her father was a convicted felon sentenced to thirty years for repeated crimes, such as identity theft and mail and bank fraud—it was much easier to tell them he'd died when she was only six years old and she never really knew him.

Because he really was dead to her. She'd had no contact with him since the feds had cuffed him right in front of her as she ate a bowl of Cap'n Crunch and watched her favorite cartoon, *As Told by Ginger*.

Despite Troy's parents' objection—and probably

because of it—the two of them had eloped to Las Vegas a week after the proposal. It was the first time Cassie had been out of the state of Florida.

She'd met Marissa the night she and Troy went out to Del Frisco's to celebrate their fifth anniversary. Marissa was their server, giving them free dessert and a champagne toast to celebrate their milestone. Complimenting Cassie on her beauty. They'd bonded over their mutual love of fashion and had become fast friends.

Two years after Marissa had walked into Cassie's life, she walked out with Troy.

Cassie opened another one of the wardrobe boxes and reconfirmed that pretty dresses were much better company than duplicitous friends. She grabbed an armful of fabric and lifted the garments off the box's metal bar. As she started to walk toward the bed to deposit them, something caught her eye at the bottom of the box.

She did a double take and saw the missing black garment bag lying crumpled at the bottom of the box. It must've slipped off the hanging bar and fallen to the bottom. That's why she hadn't seen it until she'd unpacked and hung the clothing in her closet.

She dropped the dozen or so dresses she held in her arms and grabbed the garment bag, unzipping it and peeling it away to reveal her lucky dress. The tags were still on it.

"There you are!" she squealed and hugged the dress to her. "I thought I'd lost you forever."

After her bitter trip down memory lane remembering Marissa and Troy's betrayal, Cassie knew this was a sure sign that life was getting better.

"Who needs them when I have my dresses and you, Luna?"

The little dog threw her head back and did one of her yodel-barks as if seconding the notion.

"And Gabby, too," Cassie added as she hung the dress up, slipping the metal hook of the hanger over the door so she could assess the wrinkles. "We have each other."

Even though Gabby was still in Orlando and she was in Tinsley Cove. She desperately wanted to talk to her sister, but she knew she'd have a hard time keeping quiet about the possibility of Gabby filming a scene with her. It was too exciting. As soon as Dalton gave the official nod, she would call Gabby and invite her to come up.

As Cassie picked up the dresses off the bedroom floor, someone knocked at the door. Luna jumped up and raced to the back door, barking like a fierce watchdog three times her size.

It was probably Sophie coming over to see if she could pry more deets out of her on what had happened in the driveway last night. When they'd heard her voice, they'd moved apart. By the time Sophie had walked around the truck to where they were,

Logan was sitting behind the wheel. He mentioned that he had come over to explain to Cassie that he'd been talking to Lorraine and Bob Holmes.

After he'd pulled out of the driveway, Cassie said she was exhausted and was going to call it a night. Sophie hadn't pressed the issue, but Cassie wasn't sure whether or not Sophie had seen her hugging Logan. As she flung open the door, prepared to head off any conversation about last night by leading with the saga of her lost and found lucky dress—to her surprise, it wasn't Sophie.

Logan was standing there.

Oh, yes! was her first thought.

Immediately followed by *Oooh, crap.*

She didn't have on a stitch of makeup. Her hair was piled on top of her head in a messy bun. Since this was supposed to be a lazy day, she hadn't bothered to put on a bra under the T-shirt she'd paired with her bike shorts.

Okay, well, hello there, Logan, welcome to the real me.

"Good, you're home. Sorry to just pop in, but I have fabulous news," he said as Luna ran circles around him. "I didn't want to deflate it by texting you and saying I have good news."

He was holding something behind his back.

"What is it?" she asked, crossing her arms over her chest. "I mean, come in."

She motioned him inside. As soon as he stepped

through the door, he pulled out a bottle of champagne with a flourish and a satisfied smile.

"What is this for?" she asked.

"It's for us," he said. "Get some glasses."

She didn't have champagne glasses. Since they'd eloped, Troy's mother had thought it would be gauche to register for wedding gifts. The few pieces of expensive crystal and china his parents had given them had stayed with Troy because they'd been family heirlooms. But she did have wineglasses.

"You do realize it's only ten forty-five, right?" she asked as she took the glasses from the cupboard and held each one up to the light to make sure they were smudge-free.

Truth be told, she'd drink champagne with him at any hour.

He followed her into the kitchen and dislodged the cork with a low, steady hiss, smiling the entire time. What on earth was happening? Maybe her pep talk last night had worked...

"Are you going to fill me in?" she asked as he poured the golden bubbly into the glasses and handed one to her.

"I would like to propose a toast to the dynamic duo of Sandcastle Real Estate," he said, touching his glass to hers. "I just wrote a contract on Broadhurst House. The buyers want the place and all the furniture."

"That's fabulous, Logan. Congratulations!"

She was mentally high-fiving herself because he'd come over here to celebrate this moment with her. This was going somewhere. It was kind of thrilling, actually.

"Cassie, a large part of why the fifteen-million-dollar house sold at asking price after being on the market for such a short time was because of how you staged it."

"No," Cassie said. "Maybe dressing it up helped, but it takes a skilled salesperson to help buyers see themselves in a home with a price tag like that."

Logan shook his head. "We picked up the listing after another firm couldn't sell it and the owners lost confidence. The house sat empty the whole time the other agency had it. Then you come in and work your magic. So, I'm toasting you."

They clinked glasses and sipped.

"You know what else that means," Logan said. "You're going to get a cut of the commission. You earned it."

"Oh my gosh," Cassie said as she mentally calculated the percentage she and Bert had agreed on. It would be a check for nearly five figures.

"Oh my gosh," she said again, more exuberantly. Glass in hand, she threw her arms around Logan's neck, accidently sloshing a little champagne on his cheek in the process.

"I'm so sorry." She set her glass down on the counter and leaned in to wipe his cheek. While she did that, Logan leaned closer and pressed his lips to hers.

It started as a whisper of a kiss that made her heart pound and her body say, *whoa*.

It progressed slowly. A brush of lips. A hint of tongue. Testing the waters. When she slid her arms around his neck and opened her mouth, giving him permission, he pulled her closer and deepened the kiss.

Cassie fisted her hands in his hair and pulled their bodies closer, breast to chest, suddenly glad she hadn't bothered with the bra.

She'd forgotten how good it felt to be in a man's arms.

Had it ever been *this* good?

This kiss was electric. Shock waves coursed through her.

Logan's hands slid over her back, down her waist until he cupped her bottom and pulled her into him, making her entire body vibrate. Every single one of her senses was heightened, as if she had just awakened from a long sleep.

Oooh, yes.

Now, not only was she awake, but she was alive.

Just beneath the sound of her pulse pounding in her ears, the ragged edge of Logan's breath hitched, and he pulled her even closer.

And the smell of him…clean like soap. Earthy like cedar… Masculine like him. It was him and it was becoming so familiar…something she looked forward to. Something she needed as much as the air she breathed.

This heady new discovery…the way he tasted—of mint and champagne and something else that was hard to pin down. It teased her senses…made her drunk with pleasure. It made her feel hot and sexy and just a little bit reckless.

She tugged at his shirt until it broke free from the waistband of his pants. She slid both hands underneath, reveling in the smooth, hot feel of his skin.

He followed her lead and slid his hands beneath her T-shirt, up her sides and around front to her breasts.

As they teased and tasted, the last bit of rationale she possessed took flight.

She wanted him. If she didn't have him right now, she might melt into a pool of molten lava right here on the kitchen floor.

Admitting that to herself, giving herself permission to want this man, made her body sing and burn even hotter… Even though there was an urgency, she forced herself to slow down and lose herself in him. To savor every single moment…the smell and the taste of him…the feel of his body, rock hard and fabulous, under her hands, committing it to memory…the achingly beautiful feel of his work-roughened hands on her sensitive bare breasts. She was tempted to lose the T-shirt and rid him of his polo…

until something that didn't belong nudged its way into her consciousness.

It was music. A low but determined hum sounding over the blood rushing in her ears. A familiar tune, but it didn't belong here.

Not now.

It was an electronic version of Justin Timberlake's "SexyBack"... Gabby's ringtone. Cassie tried to ignore it and, miraculously, it finally went away...but only for a moment before it started back up.

"What is that?" Logan asked, pulling away, looking disoriented as he glanced around the kitchen.

Cassie pressed both hands to her face. It was flaming hot.

"That's my sister, Gabby. Or, I mean, that's her ringtone."

"Go ahead and get it," he said as he tucked his shirt back into his pants.

The song stopped, but the spell was broken.

Then it started for a third time.

"Are you serious right now?" she cried at the phone, which was lying on the kitchen counter right where she'd left it when she'd been checking her social media while she ate her breakfast.

"Seriously, you'd better get that. It might be important."

He was inching toward the back door.

"Just hold on a sec," Cassie said. "I'll tell her I'll call her back."

He waved her off. "No, really, I've got to run. I... um... I know you've got things to do. I've already stayed too long. I just wanted to share the good news."

She was ready to tell him that she would not allow him to make that electric kiss weird. Not after he'd come over here unannounced with a bottle of champagne, enticing her into day drinking and dangling the promise of hot sex that he had no intention of delivering.

Despite her inner bravado, all she could manage was "Logan, don't go."

But as Justin Timberlake started another chorus about bringing sexy back, Logan was already out the door.

What the hell was wrong with him?

By Monday morning, Logan had lost count of how many times he'd asked himself that question. He still hadn't figured out the answer.

He cursed himself under his breath.

"You're in a good mood," Sophie said as she poured herself a cup of coffee. "What's wrong with you?"

"Nothing's wrong with me," he growled.

"I'd hate to see your demeanor if something was the matter," Sophie said.

"I just have a lot on my mind."

"*Ohh*, does any of it have to do with a certain blonde who lives next door to me? After what I saw on Saturday night, I was hoping that you'd have a spring in your step this morning."

"I don't know what you think you saw, but when you came over and poked your nose into our business on Saturday, I told you I went to Cassie's to explain why I'd disappeared before we went onstage. Sorry to disappoint you, but there was nothing to see there."

He focused his attention on pouring himself a cup of coffee, hoping that Sophie hadn't seen his truck parked in Cassie's driveway yesterday morning. Or worse yet, that Cassie hadn't gone next door and lamented to his sister about what a jerk he was for kissing and running.

"Okay, moody, whatever," Sophie said. As she walked away, he thought he heard her mutter under her breath that it might do him some good to get laid.

That was the point. Since Natalie died, he'd had a handful of one-night stands, thinking they might melt away his icy numbness, but each one had only made him feel worse. He would not use Cassie that way. He'd known her two weeks, and he already recognized that she was special. She deserved better than an irreparably broken louse who kissed her and ran because he couldn't handle it.

Before they got down to business, he would apologize for losing control yesterday and assure her it would never happen again.

The entire cast was scheduled to shoot a scene in the Sandcastle conference room revolving around a weekly staff meeting, where Logan was supposed to present the good news about the contract on Broadhurst House. As far as he knew, his father had never held weekly staff meetings, since they would involve only him, Owen, Forest and possibly Sophie. But the addition of the meeting was Dalton's brainchild. It was an easy opportunity for the whole cast to come together for a group scene.

Logan just wanted to get the shoot over with. He had things he had to do today. He was driving over to Figure Eight Island to meet with a couple about listing their house—a lead from the Broadhurst owners—and he was taking a buyer from New York around to see some vacation homes.

He was kind of amazed at how well this temporary gig selling houses was going.

Now, if he could just set things right with Cassie so they could have a clean slate and focus on working together to stage and sell houses.

He glanced around to see if she had arrived yet, but there was no sign of her. He checked his watch. It was fifteen minutes until call time. Normally she was early.

He hoped she wasn't avoiding him because of yesterday.

He stepped out of the conference room on his way to the supply room to pick up a couple of folios for client papers when he saw Cassie standing at the brand-new reception desk that had been installed to dress up the office for filming. She was talking to Lucy.

He needed to rip off the bandage and apologize. He caught Cassie's eye as he approached and she turned her attention to her phone.

"Good morning," he said.

"Hey, Logan," Lucy said. "Sorry, I need to run and put on another pot of coffee. Dalton is paying me extra to work craft services today."

As soon as Lucy disappeared into the conference room, he said, "How are you?"

"I'm fine, thank you." Cassie's gaze was trained on her phone, and she kept tap-tapping away. Last week, he might've thought she was just busy, but he heard a distinct note in her voice that let him know he'd crossed a line.

This was going to be harder than he'd hoped, but what had he expected?

"I owe you an apology for yesterday," he said. "It shouldn't have happened. I'm sorry it did. I'm in no place to get involved, and I don't want to lead you on."

She looked up from her phone and regarded him with a neutral expression that he couldn't read. His mouth went dry.

"I'm not looking to get involved, either," she said. "So, no sweat. Now, if you'll excuse me, I need to finish this before Dalton calls us to the set."

She turned her attention back to her phone.

He stood there for a moment wishing he had the words to make this right. Or better yet, wishing he could go back to yesterday and have a do-over.

He knew that life didn't offer do-overs.

As he walked away, a little voice deep down said that no matter how much he regretted not being able to give her what she deserved, he'd liked the kiss.

Maybe he wasn't completely dead after all, but now wasn't the time to test that theory.

"Boys and girls, listen up." Dalton clapped his hands twice. "I need everyone in the conference room for announcements before we start filming. We will start in two minutes. So *vite, vite!*"

Logan sat down first. Cassie chose a chair next to his mother, a few spaces down from him on the same side of the table. Bunny and Owen were between them. If Logan wanted to see her, he'd have to lean in and crane his neck. He wouldn't do that. He could take a hint.

Dalton stood at the head of the table. Logan was to his left.

"Welcome to the third week of shooting, everyone," Dalton said. "The crew and I are tickled pink with how the show is taking shape. We were able to get into the editing booth yesterday and have a look at this week's footage. We've got a good thing going here, people. Keep up the good work."

Excited murmurs rippled through the room. Logan wished he could see Cassie. He thought about leaning forward and looking at her because maybe it would break the ice, but before he could, Dalton said, "I have a question for Logan and Cassie."

The room fell silent.

Logan knew what he was going to say before he said it.

"On Saturday night, Cassie's doorbell cam caught Logan going in the front door, but Logan, you never came out. What's going on there, folks? Do we have a budding romance after all?"

Hopeful sounds ricocheted through the room. A female voice, maybe Lucy, stage-whispered, "I hope so." Logan had been looking down, so he couldn't see who said it.

After all that went down yesterday, this was not helpful.

"Can you stop pushing the romance?" Logan said. "In some workplaces it would be grounds for harassment."

After the room fell silent, he wished he'd kept his mouth shut. Everything he said or did seemed to dig him deeper into it. He tried to cover by saying, "I'm sitting here now. Obviously, there's something wrong with the camera."

Dalton clasped his hands in front of him.

"Yeah, about that harassment comment. We're not here to force anyone into situations that make them uncomfortable. But romance sells. If anyone is feeling compromised, please see me after the shoot today. We will work something out. Having said that, I do need to let Logan and Cassie know that we were able to score a last-minute booking for you for tomorrow night on the live late-night show *Look What's Happening Now* to do some prepublicity for *Selling Sandcastle*. They're recording on location in Savannah. You'll be on with a few of the cast members from *Charmed, Savannah*.

"If this trip is going to be a problem for anyone— if it makes anyone uncomfortable—I need to know right now."

Dalton looked pointedly at Cassie.

"No problem here," she said, but she didn't sound happy about it.

"I'm there," said Logan.

"Good," said Dalton. "You leave tomorrow morning. Zoe is setting up your transportation and accommodations."

Chapter Eleven

"Hey, guess where I am?" Cassie said when Gabby answered the phone. "You'll never guess."

"*Hmm*…let's see…are you at the Postal Museum in Vaduz, Liechtenstein?" Gabby asked.

"What? No. Is that even a real place?" Cassie said.

"Of course it's a real place. Do you think I'd make up something like that?"

"Well, that was random."

"I read an article about it last week," Gabby said. "What do you expect me to say when you say I'll never guess? It had to be somewhere outlandish."

"I'm sure Liechtenstein's Postal Museum is fascinating, so good guess, but wrong," Cassie said. "I'm in Savannah, Georgia, getting ready to be on the *Look What's Happening Now* show to promote *Selling Sandcastle*. Can you believe it?"

"Hold up," Gabby said. "You're really going to be on *Look What's Happening Now*? The one with Mikey Biggs?"

"Yes."

Cassie had to hold the phone away from her ear as Gabby squealed loudly.

"Shut up, Cassie. Are you kidding me? You know how much I love that show. But they usually do that show in New York. Why are they in Savannah, and more importantly, why didn't you get me in to watch the filming?"

"You know I would've if I could have," Cassie said. "I just found out about this yesterday. We're going to be on *Look What's Happening Now* with some of the cast from the show *Charmed, Savannah*. We're promoting *Selling Sandcastle*. Will you please set the DVR to record it? Though I don't know if I can watch myself on television— Oh, gosh, what if I say something stupid?"

"You will do great. But you said, '*we're* going to be on.' Who is *we*?"

"I'm here with one of my cast mates, Logan McFadden."

"Ooh, is he pretty?" Gabby asked.

Cassie considered telling Gabby how her ill-timed phone call on Sunday had interrupted a kiss that had curled her toes and made her lady parts sing, but if she did, that meant that she'd have to backtrack and tell her sister how Logan had sprinted out of her house like a jackrabbit.

She hadn't mentioned it on Sunday when she'd finally picked up Gabby's call. When her sister had asked why she sounded so annoyed, she'd said she'd been napping. Standing there with the phone pressed to her ear, she could still feel his lips on hers and his hands on her body.

Remembering the humiliating scene and how he'd apologized yesterday made her cringe. They'd flown to Savannah together today, but they'd barely said two words to each other on the short flight. After they'd gotten to the hotel, she'd gone to her room and she wasn't sure what he'd done with his time. That was his business.

She got up off the bed and walked to the window to gaze out over the park.

"Yeah, he's okay, I guess. But you know what's really pretty? This hotel. They've put us up in the Mansion hotel on Forsyth Park. It used to be the Lewis Kayton House before they remodeled it into a hotel. Lots of history."

"I've heard about that place. It's supposed to be something else."

"It lives up to its reputation. It even has an art gallery in it. Tonight, we're taping *Look What's Happening Now* in the park right next to the famous Forsyth

Fountain. I'm looking out the window and I can see them setting up now."

"My sister is going to be famous," Gabby said. "That's so darn cool."

"Well, since I couldn't get you up here in time to see *Look What's Happening Now*, how about if I made it up to you by flying you up to Tinsley Cove so that you can film a couple of scenes from *Selling Sandcastle*?"

Gabby went so quiet that Cassie thought they'd been disconnected.

"Gabs, are you there?"

"I'm here. I think we might have a bad connection, because I thought you just said I could be on your television show."

"I did. For a couple of scenes, anyway. The producer told us we could come up with our own scene and we could choose who we wanted to film with, and I chose you."

Gabby let out an ear-piercing squeal. "Shut up! Shut up! Shut up! OMG, I am so happy. When?"

"It's going to be soon. Like maybe next week. Can you make that work?"

"You know I can. I will move mountains to make it work."

In some ways Cassie felt bad that she was the one that Dalton had plucked from the throngs of people who had auditioned for the cooking competition. This was so much more up Gabby's alley than it was hers. After all, Gabby was the one who had pulled her into the initial audition, but her sister had been gracious and Cassie was trying to learn how to accept opportunities as they materialized rather than believing that she had to take a back seat to everyone else.

"I should know more about when we will film later this week, after I get back from Savannah. Right now, I'd better run. Unlike *Selling Sandcastle*, *Look What's Happening Now* has hair and makeup people to help us look our best. I need to find out when they'll be ready for me."

"You are gorgeous every single day, with or without a glam squad. I'm so proud of you, little sis."

After they hung up, Cassie picked up the information packet that had been waiting for her in her room, along with a fruit basket and a bottle of wine to welcome her. She peeled a banana and ate it sitting on the bed as she looked over the itinerary.

The glam squad would come to her. In the meantime, she had about two hours to kill. She was contemplating going out for a walk when her room phone rang.

"Hello?"

"Hey, Cassie. It's Logan."

Her stomach flipped and then dipped in disappointment in herself for her visceral reaction to the sound of his voice.

"Hello." She thought about being cheeky and asking him if he was calling to ask if he could borrow a banana, to which she would reply, *No, I'm keeping all the bananas to myself,* but that sounded too friendly and vaguely sexual. Instead, she said nothing.

"We have a couple of hours before we have to be anywhere—or at least that's how they have me scheduled—if you're not busy, I was hoping we could talk. Maybe have a glass of wine or coffee or something. I hate the way things are between us, and I'd like to break the ice before we have to go on live national TV."

Her stomach clenched at the thought of being on live TV. She'd known it. That's what *Look What's Happening Now* was all about, the live interview. But it hadn't had a chance to register until now. In a way, Logan was right.

"I guess the last thing we need is to look like a couple of awkward, sullen duds on national television."

She knew that was kind of a mean dig, but he deserved it after kissing her so thoroughly—and making her like it—then walking out and telling her it never should've happened.

The way she saw it, she had two choices: they could talk or she could hang up on him right now and make him sweat. But that might make him think she was bitter. He'd hurt her feelings, but she wasn't bitter. She wasn't built that way. After what had happened with Troy and Marissa, she knew she needed to grow a stronger backbone and not let people take her for granted.

Even so, having a plan would be better. It would be the professional thing to do.

Plus, Logan was the one who had reached out to her.

"I'll meet you down in the bar in fifteen minutes," she said and hung up.

Logan arrived at the lobby bar and chose a seat in the corner next to the window.

It was late afternoon, and the place was empty except for a couple of guys drinking bourbon at the bar. Logan heard them order when he walked by.

One wall was lined with arched floor-to-ceiling windows. Despite the natural light, the bar, with its wood floors and dark furniture—some leather, some upholstered—was dim. The deep green faux marble wallpaper might've had something to do with the low light quality. When he looked again, he couldn't tell if the wallpaper was marble or a blurry depiction of the Spanish moss–laden live oak boughs that seemed to be the trademark of the area.

A grandfather clock near his seat chimed four times. The two guys at the bar clinked their tumblers and knocked back the brown liquor. They laughed at something the woman behind the bar said.

As she poured them another round, Cassie entered the bar, and both guys turned to look at her.

"Good afternoon," drawled the blond in a lazy, bourbon-laced Southern accent.

"Hello," Cassie said as she passed. She stopped to do a double take. "I know you two. Aren't you Greg and Beau from *Charmed, Savannah*?"

"Yes, ma'am," said the guy with brown hair. "What is your name, gorgeous, and better yet, will you please let us buy you a drink?"

An inexplicable dark twist of emotion had Logan clenching his fists under the table. He knew he had no right to feel territorial. Cassie was free to have a drink with anyone she wanted, but he still felt a little jealous.

As he tried to process what he was feeling, she said, "I'm Cassie Houston, from the show *Selling Sandcastle*." She gestured toward the corner of the bar. "Logan McFadden and I are going to be on *Look What's Happening Now* with the two of you tonight."

"Well, then y'all both need to join us for a drink," said the blond.

The two got up and walked with Cassie to the table where Logan was sitting.

"Beau Weatherly," said the blond. "Nice to meet you, Logan. Cassie says you're joining us on *Look What's Happening Now* tonight. Greg and I want to buy y'all a drink to welcome you to Savannah."

Logan had never seen the show *Charmed, Savannah*, but he'd looked it up after he'd gotten to the hotel. Now, he recognized Beau and Greg from the cast photo. From what he'd read, it seemed that the two were notorious for living large and loving the ladies.

That put what he was feeling into perspective. He wanted to protect Cassie. Though he had a feeling that she would take issue with that and tell him she didn't need to be protected, it never hurt to have someone looking out for you.

That's why he wanted to say, *no, thanks*. In addition to looking out for Cassie, there were several reasons for wanting to decline: he didn't want to drink before going on live television, and with the two of them sitting here, he wouldn't get to talk to Cassie. But they still had several hours before the cameras would start rolling and everyone was already making themselves comfortable—Cassie sat beside Logan on the banquette, while the guys sat in the chairs across the table. The bartender was at the ready to take their orders.

When Cassie ordered a glass of champagne, Greg said, "Make it a bottle of Veuve. We need to have a toast."

He and Beau also ordered another round of bourbon. When they pressed Logan to join them, he said, "I'm good. I'll stick with the champagne."

After the drinks were delivered and they'd dispensed with the basic small talk about where they were from and what the show *Selling Sandcastle* was about, Beau started putting the moves on Cassie.

"Has anyone ever told you that you have the most beautiful eyes?" he slurred. "I'm sure you hear it all the time, because you do."

"That's very sweet of you," Cassie replied.

Again, Logan found his hands fisting under the table. He flexed his fingers and laid his palms flat out on the table. Cassie did have beautiful eyes. It was one of the first things he'd noticed about her, even if he hadn't vocalized it like Bourbon Beau.

She deserved to hear compliments.

Beau refilled Cassie's glass.

"A toast to beautiful eyes," he said, touching his glass to hers. "There's a party tonight after the show wraps. Why don't you come?"

"Thank you, but we have an early flight home in the morning," she said. "I'd better not."

Beau put his forearms on the table and leaned across the table toward her. "I'll take you to the airport in the morning myself. I must see you tonight. I am smitten."

"Oh, well." Cassie laughed nervously and shifted in her seat, placing both hands flat on the banquette. Before Logan could think better of it, he put his hand on top of hers and gave it a quick, gentle squeeze. She grabbed his hand, lacing her fingers through his, and put it on the table.

"I do appreciate the offer, but…" She nodded toward their entwined hands.

"Oh, whoa, dude, sorry." Beau sat back in his chair

so fast it was as if someone had pushed him. "I didn't mean to encroach. You're a hell of a lucky guy."

Greg made a scribbling sign in the air, letting the bartender know to cash them out.

"It was great to meet you…both," said Beau. "We need to run. We will catch you tonight at the show."

The two stumbled out of the hotel and onto Drayton Street, leaving Cassie and Logan alone in the bar. Her hand was still in his. She hadn't moved away to reclaim her personal space.

Logan remembered that day at Broadhurst House when her hand felt so natural in his. Just like it did now.

"I know you can handle yourself, but I hope you know that I'm here for you," Logan said. "Always."

Cassie slid her hand away and crossed her arms.

"I keep thinking about how I ran out on Sunday and…" He laced his hands in front of him on the table. "I'm sorry."

"You've already apologized. You don't have to keep doing that."

"What I mean is, I'm *sorry*. I'm sorry I freaked out. I'm so sorry I hurt you. This is new territory for me, Cassie. I don't really know what I'm doing."

He hadn't planned on telling her this, but as he heard the words flowing out of his mouth…out of his heart, he knew they were spot-on.

He didn't want to lose her. He couldn't lose her.

He had no idea what he was doing, but he knew he had to do something to make things right.

He slanted a look at her. She was watching him intently. He turned to face her.

"Beau was right," he said. "You do have the most beautiful eyes. But what he doesn't know and I do know is that you also have the most incredible spirit and the kindest heart. You make me laugh, and I was sure I'd never be able to laugh again. Cassie, when I'm with you—when I hold you—I feel like it just might be possible to be whole again. My problem is I don't know how to get from here to there. I'm a little rusty at this. Do you think you can bear with me and give me another chance?"

Chapter Twelve

"Don't keep me hanging," Gabby said. "Did you sleep with him?"

Gabby had barely gotten settled into Cassie's house after arriving for her guest appearance on *Selling Sandcastle* when she demanded that her sister tell her everything.

"I mean, come on, the guy is gorgeous, Cass. I noticed that first thing when I saw you on *Look What's Happening Now*. So, you're in a romantic hotel, in a romantic city, just the two of you. Please tell me at least a little hanky-panky went down."

Cassie smiled to herself as she weighed her words. "No, I didn't sleep with him in Savannah. We're taking things slowly."

Gabby pulled a face that looked like she smelled something, but before she could follow up with a grilling, Cassie said, "It's good, Gabs. We're building something really good here. We're working through some emotional baggage, and neither of us wants to ruin this thing."

As she stood at the breakfast bar in the kitchen arranging meat, cheese and crackers for a charcuterie board snack to enjoy with the bottle of red wine Cassie had picked up for Gabby's visit, she thought about telling her sister about the missteps she and Logan had made along the way, but there was no point in rehashing the past when she was focusing on moving forward.

"You do seem really happy, and I'm happy for you." Gabby took a sip of wine. "So, since you're in such a good space, I need to tell you something."

Cassie recognized the note in her sister's voice. Whatever she had to say wasn't good.

"What's wrong?" she asked as she put the last piece of cheese in place.

"If you're finished with that—" Gabby nodded to the board "—could we bring it in the living room and get comfortable?"

"Sure."

Cassie grabbed her wine and carried the board into the living room. Her heart thudded as she went through the mental list of any possible things that be bad news.

"Okay, what is it?" she said. "Are you okay?"

Gabby waved away Cassie's concern as she settled herself on the sofa next to her sister.

"I'm fine," Gabby said. "But… Technically, I know I shouldn't tell you this, but you're my favorite sister." She flashed a wide, toothy smile at Cassie. "I could never throw you to the wolves…"

Gabby took a piece of salami and cheese and set them atop a cracker.

"If you take a bite of that without telling me what's going on, I'm going to throw this whole board away."

Gabby set her cracker creation down on the cocktail napkin Cassie had provided.

"I got a call from someone named Seth who works on the show…"

Cassie nodded. "Right, Seth is one of the production assistants."

"He told me that I needed to bring a bombshell that was supposed to be revealed to you during the filming, but I couldn't do that to you, so you're going to have to act totally surprised when we get to that portion of the program."

Cassie knitted her brows. "Thank you for telling me, but is there a bombshell?"

This time Gabby did take a bite of her salami and cheese cracker, and she took her time chewing it. Cassie didn't hurry her because, frankly, she wasn't sure she wanted to know about this *bombshell*.

"All right, I don't know how else to tell you this,

so I'll just say it. Troy and Marissa are getting married."

"Oh." Cassie took a gulp of wine and braced herself for the assault of feelings that were bound to pierce her heart. Funny enough, they didn't come.

She shrugged. "Of course they are."

"From what I hear, Marissa is pregnant."

This part was more annoying, because clearly Marissa would stoop to any level to get what she wanted. "Good for her. It's what she always wanted. Now she'll have two babies on her hands—Troy and his spawn."

"You know he wouldn't have married her if not for the baby."

"I don't know," said Cassie. "I never thought he would have an affair with my best friend, but he did. I don't know what to believe anymore."

They sat in silence eating and sipping.

"Did you run this little ditty by Seth?" Cassie asked. "Is it legal for you to talk about this on television? They can't turn around and sue the show or us for it, can they?"

"I told them. So I guess it's for them and their legal team to decide. At least the show's not live. So if they think it might be a problem, they can always cut it." She frowned. "And there goes my television debut."

Little by little the numbness was starting to give way to another feeling she couldn't quite place.

After all that had happened with Troy, she didn't want him back, but there was a twinge of…of what? Envy, maybe, that Marissa was having a child and she wasn't. Of course, if Cassie and Troy had had a child, it would've made the divorce even messier rather than the clean break it had been. Still, ever since she'd lost her mother, she'd felt that the only way to get back that safe-harbor feeling of family was to have a child of her own.

She tried to take comfort in how things were progressing with Logan, but maybe she shouldn't cocoon herself in a relationship that was still so tentative. A hollowness rang through her. A family of her own had never seemed as out of her reach as it did right now.

"There's one more thing," Gabby said.

"I'm going to send you back to Orlando if you keep lobbing bad news at me."

Gabby smiled and nodded. "I know, right? I feel like the bringer of gloom and doom, but this one isn't quite so bad, depending on how you look at it."

"Just tell me," Cassie said.

"I got a call from Dad."

The bottom dropped out of Cassie's stomach, and for a minute she couldn't speak.

"Apparently, he got released early. He had been sentenced to thirty years. He's served twenty-one. He got time off for good behavior or something like that.

I didn't ask him to elaborate. I thought you should know that he asked me for your number."

"You didn't give it to him, did you?"

"Of course not. I didn't tell him anything about you except that I needed to talk to you before I gave him any information about you."

"After all these years, what does he want? He never called or sent a single birthday note or paid a cent of child support, and Mom worked herself into an early grave because it."

Cassie felt bile slowly rising in the back of her throat.

"I know," Gabby said. "But he said he'd like to see us if we're open to it."

Cassie shook her head.

"No. Absolutely not. And Gabby, you can't tell anyone about this. I told everyone here that our father is dead because I didn't want to explain. I didn't want to be looked at as the daughter of a man who bilked innocent people out of their life savings. He is dead to me."

Gabby's eyes mirrored Cassie's sadness.

"Keep in mind that he found out how to contact me and be prepared. Because he sounded pretty determined."

Located about a mile and a half from the beach, downtown Tinsley Cove looked like a movie set. Main Street was a ten-block collection of eclectic buildings—a mix of brightly colored beachy-casual wooden structures and stone-and-brick European charmers lining a stretch of cobblestoned road.

For their filming adventure, Gabby, Sophie and Cassie went shopping in the boutiques downtown. They capped off the morning with lunch at the Garden Café, where Gabby broke the news to Cassie that her ex was getting married. She claimed that she'd come up because she wanted to break the news in person and not over the phone.

Grateful that Gabby had given her the heads-up last night, Cassie did her best not to scoff and roll her eyes. Instead, she acted surprised, projecting just enough pensive melancholy to make Dalton believe that she was hearing the news for the first time.

Dalton seemed to buy it, and so did Logan, who showed up to watch the filming of the lunch scene from the sidelines.

"You okay?" he asked as Sophie and Gabby chatted with Dalton.

Not wanting to take a chance on anyone overhearing her, Cassie whispered, "I'm fine. The girls and I are going to the Rusty Anchor tonight to celebrate Gabby's film debut and her last night here. Want to join us? I'll fill you in then."

He hesitated. "I don't want to get in the middle of a girls' night out."

"I wouldn't have invited you if you weren't welcome. Are you coming or not? I really hope you will."

She smiled at him, and her gaze dropped to his lips. She bit down on her own bottom lip, because that was exactly what she wanted to do to him, but not here in front of everyone. They had been taking it slowly since reaching their Savannah peace treaty.

Between their filming schedules, Logan's burgeoning real estate career and Gabby coming into town, there hadn't been a lot of time to sneak off together. And it would be sneaking since, for the time being, they'd decided to keep things on the down low until they sorted out their feelings.

"Good," he said. "I'm dying to see you."

Logan picked them up at seven thirty and drove them to the Rusty Anchor, which was located on the Intracoastal Waterway. The bar's rough-hewn edges had aged to a glorious patina that gave the impression that the place could've been there as long as the dunes had lined the beach.

On the way over, Sophie had warned Gabby that it wasn't a glamorous place, but it was fresh and fun and she would definitely have a good time because a lot of hot guys hung out there.

"The locals come here for the fresh catch and a fun place to dance," she said. "Places like this earn their keep by offering good fresh food, cold beer and live music out on the open deck. If it was dirty or served anything but the best seafood, it wouldn't be as packed as it is tonight."

Logan parked his truck in front of a tall palm tree on the far side of the crowded parking lot.

The minute she stepped out of the truck, Cassie heard music playing. She breathed in the scent of a wood-fired grill mingling with the marsh, beer and something delicious.

Anticipation washed over Cassie as she realized this was the first time she and Logan had had a real night out together. Even if they weren't alone, there was a decidedly different feel in the air.

As they walked the length of the dock, beneath the market lights strung overhead, a gentle breeze blew in off the water, making her tip her face up.

Sunburned people danced and clustered around newspaper-covered tables, drinking beer from bottles and eating oysters and peel-it-yourself shrimp.

At the far end of the deck, a guy playing acoustic guitar sat on a stool, strumming and singing the Zac Brown Band song "Knee Deep" into a microphone on a stand.

The music floated over the convivial sound of people laughing and talking. The party had obviously been going on for a while, but the music and the unpretentious, beachy atmosphere made it easy to fall right in.

It made her smile.

"This way." Logan surprised her by grabbing her

hand and navigating through the throngs of people. The unselfconscious way he linked his fingers through hers—in front of Gabby and Sophie—made her heart bloom.

Every table was taken, so they stopped near the wooden railing, a few feet away from the singer.

"I'm guessing you've been here before?" she asked.

"A time or two," he said. "Another lifetime ago."

Cassie wondered if he'd come here with Natalie, but she pushed away the thought.

"Gabby and I will go get us some drinks," Sophie said, smiling as she glanced at her brother's hand in Cassie's.

Cassie suddenly felt shy and tempted to pull away but quickly decided that would be a dumb move.

This was the most openly affectionate Logan had ever been. Why would she want to spoil it?

They decided to get a bucket of beer. Logan gave Sophie his credit card and told her to start a tab. Their sisters left them alone in the crowd and made their way toward the bar, which was situated just inside the tin-roofed portion of the shanty.

The singer shifted into a Jimmy Buffett song that was somewhere in the murky middle between fast and slow.

On the makeshift dance floor—which was really just the center of the deck—sun-kissed men and women attempted to dance to the music, moving their bodies with beers in hand and arms over their heads. Some swayed while others shuffled and stomped, moving around each other in what looked like a primal mating ritual.

As Cassie and Logan watched, the party at the four-top table next to where they were standing got up to leave, and a guy motioned them over.

It was prime real estate—overlooking the water, right up against the deck railing.

"Are you always this lucky?" Cassie asked as Logan pulled out a chair for her.

He leaned in and whispered in her ear, "I guess that remains to be seen." Her stomach turned upside down at the innuendo.

After they seated themselves, Logan and Cassie sitting next to each other, he asked, "So, your ex is getting married? How do you feel about that?"

Cassie shrugged. "I wish them well. They deserve each other."

She told him how Dalton had asked Gabby to drop the bombshell on her while they were filming but that her sister had forewarned her.

"She knows better than that," Cassie said. "It's one of those things that stings a little when you hear it, but after you have a minute to digest it, you realize it's very freeing."

Gabby and Sophie preempted the conversation when they arrived with the bucket of beers, setting it on the table with a thud.

Logan pulled an icy bottle from the bunch, popped the cap and handed it to Cassie. As he passed it to her, he smiled, and a sensual feeling in the pit of her stomach unfurled.

He opened ones for Gabby and Sophie before helping himself and holding his bottle up in cheers. They clinked bottles and took long draws of the beer.

Cassie couldn't remember when something tasted so good…except for the afternoon that Logan had kissed her.

The singer moved into a rowdy set of country tunes. The volume seemed to increase more than a few decibels. Gabby and Sophie took their drinks to the dance floor.

Logan slid his arm around her shoulder. "I like a woman who's not too dainty to drink her beer straight up like this."

Cassie took another sip from the bottle and licked her lips.

"Oh, yeah? Well, I like a guy who isn't afraid to crash a girls' night at a divey beach bar."

His laugh, soothing and rich, transcended the music. Then he smiled that smile that was beginning to feel like it had been made just for her.

They tried to talk over the music but finally give up on conversation, opting for watching people and communicating through glances and smiles. Cassie liked the comfort that came from not needing to talk all the time.

She sank into the feeling that they could just be.

Sophie and Gabby were dancing with guys now. Laughing and talking and having fun.

A while later, the singer slowed things down and played the Zac Brown Band song that warned a guy not to wait so long that the woman was walking away when he's finally falling in love.

Logan leaned in. "Will you dance with me?"

When Cassie was in his arms, a rogue feeling crept up on her like a creature swimming up from murky water. It spiraled through the pit of her stomach, reminding her that she was alive.

Wrapped up in the feeling of being in his arms, the exhilarating smell of the sea breeze and the magic of the setting sun turning the night inky blue, she knew she was falling for Logan.

With the news of Troy and Marissa's wedding, it felt as if the sun had set on a long, lonely chapter of her life. The next page would be a new beginning.

Logan took her hand and gave her a twirl.

When she faced him again, her head was spinning and the full moon that was rising so gracefully over the water suddenly had a twin. She blinked several times, and the two moons finally merged back together into one.

She'd only had one beer—so she wasn't drunk. Drunk on Logan, maybe? Whatever it was, she liked the rush.

"I'm going to slow things even more," the singer said. "Grab your sweetheart. It's time to get close."

As he strummed the first strains of the song "What Hurts the Most," Cassie felt Logan stiffen in her arms. For a split second, she wanted to grab a bottle off the closest table and chuck it at the singer for conjuring Natalie's ghost.

For ruining their night.

Then Logan relaxed and pulled her tighter against him.

She buried her face in his shoulder, breathing in his scent. He rested his cheek on the top of her head. They swayed together as if they were exorcising all the demons that had threatened to keep them apart.

She wanted to stay like this forever, frozen in this moment when everything was safe and right, loving the way his body felt pressed against hers, the way his hands felt as they caressed her back.

As the song ended, he pulled back and tilted her face up so that he was gazing into her eyes. She drank him in. The smooth, tanned line of throat visible at the open collar of his blue shirt. The dark hair that had just the right amount of curl to it. The deep brown eyes that were gazing down at her with such an intensity that it sent desire shimmering through her.

She knew what was going to happen before he lowered his lips to hers.

The world melted away. She had no idea how long

they stood like that on the dance floor, but finally, he whispered, "I know it's Gabby's last night, but she and Soph seem to be having fun without us. How do you feel about getting out of here and going back to my place? I can leave my keys for Sophie and call us an Uber."

There was that smile again. It could convince her to do just about anything.

Including making her fall in love with him.

Cassie warred with herself. As much as she'd longed for this moment, she couldn't cut out on her sister.

"Not tonight. But soon," she promised him. "As soon as I put my sister on the plane."

"I'm going to be out of town for the next couple of days," he said. "Dalton wants to film Forest, Owen and me getting the listing for a property in Beaufort. I'll be back on Wednesday. Would you like to get dinner?"

Suddenly, she was starving.

The next morning, when Gabby was in the shower, Cassie's phone rang.

When she saw Troy's name and number on the display screen, she almost didn't pick up. She hadn't talked to her ex-husband since the divorce. Morbid curiosity made her grab it on the fourth ring.

"Hello?"

"Hey, honey, it's me."

Honey? He had the nerve to call her honey?

Cassie considered hanging up, but she did one better. "Who is this?"

The ensuing pause lasted so long, Cassie thought they had been disconnected.

"It's Troy." The sticky sweetness that had coated his words was gone now.

"Hello, Troy."

There was another awkward pause, as if he was waiting for her to say something or finish doing cartwheels after hearing his voice. For once in her life, she had no desire to fill the silence. He'd called. He was the one who needed to talk.

"I was calling to congratulate you. I understand that you have some exciting career news."

Cassie's mind raced, wondering how he'd found out about the show, since it hadn't aired yet.

"I saw you on the *Look What's Happening Now* show last week."

Oh, right. That explains it.

"I meant to call sooner," he said. "You know how crazy life can be."

"I do know," Cassie said. "I understand congratulations are in order for you and Marissa. Gabby told me. Have you set a date?"

"Oh, that. No date. Not yet. Though she is chomping at the bit to get to the altar."

Several quips ran through Cassie's head, ranging from *She probably wants to get there before the baby is born* to *Run, Marissa! Save yourself!* But no. She didn't want Marissa to be spared. She broke it. She bought it. Cassie wanted Marissa to have the full Troy Houston experience.

So she opted to not say anything.

"Enough about me," Troy said.

Enough about him? Since when had her ex-husband ever not wanted to talk about himself?

"I'm so proud of you, Cassie bug. You're going to be a star, babe. I always knew you would be."

Cassie bug? No. I'm sorry. You do not get to refer to me by the pet name you used to call me.

Then she realized she didn't care. He could call her whatever.

Who cares?

She didn't. It hit her like a wave, and it was the most freeing feeling.

She didn't care what Troy and Marissa did. In fact, she wished them the best in their new life together. Okay, but she had to admit that a snarky voice inside her did want to say, *Good luck with that.*

What if they were meant to be? What if they truly were soul mates? All snark aside, if they were, they deserved to be together.

Heaven knew that she and Troy had been too young to know what they wanted. They'd been together since they were fourteen years old. She'd always thought someday she would grow into his family. That after she and Troy had kids, his family would embrace her and make her feel like she was truly part of the family—the daughter they'd always wanted after having a boy child.

Eventually she'd understood that was never going to happen. The only way she was going to find her true north was to stop wishing they would love her.

"Baby, I was thinking," Troy said. "Why don't I drive up and see you? You can show me around Tinsley Cove. We could spend a little time together. It's been so long. I miss you."

It's been so long? Are you kidding? What part of divorced *don't you understand, you nimrod?*

"No, that's not going to happen, but I do wish you and Marissa all the best in your life together. Goodbye, Troy."

And just like that, Cassie let go of the baggage of her past and turned toward her future.

Chapter Thirteen

Logan took the bottle of cava out of the refrigerator and set it out on the counter to warm up a few degrees. He'd gotten back to Tinsley Cove around eleven after two days on the road with his brothers and the crew.

Before going home, he'd gone into the Vine and Cork wine shop on Main Street downtown to buy a bottle for tonight. The shop owner, Fred Humston, had suggested cava.

"If you're looking for a subtle, special touch, this is what you want."

Logan had also gone to the fish market and purchased four pounds of snow crab, plus red potatoes and green beans for dinner. For dessert, key lime chocolate truffles from the Sugar Shack, which was next door to the wine shop. Simple fare, but delicious, and Cassie had mentioned that snow crab was her favorite.

He'd considered taking her out to dinner at Le Marais, the French restaurant downtown, but that seemed too stuffy. Plus, since the show had been announced, it was hard to go anywhere without people approaching and asking questions. Good for the show's popularity, but bad when you just wanted to be alone with the woman you were falling in love with.

As it was, Connie, the owner of the Sugar Shack, was determined to find out who would be the recipient of the candy.

When Cassie knocked on the door at seven o'clock, his stomach took a strange drop, which made him place a fist on his solar plexus.

The reaction could only mean one thing: he'd missed her while he was gone.

When he opened the door, she stood there looking incredibly sexy in a pink sundress. One of the dress's sleeves had slid down to reveal a tanned and very seductive shoulder. As she glanced up at him through her lashes, he had to fist his hands at his sides to slow down and keep from touching her. Then he wasn't sure who moved first, but the next thing he knew she was in his arms and he was holding her tight and kissing her like she was his oxygen and his next breath depended on her. Without letting her go, he walked them backward into the foyer, carrying her along with him, not breaking their kiss. Somehow he managed to shut the door behind them.

When they finally came up for air, she said, "Hi. I missed you."

"I missed you, too."

Gently, he set her down and watched as she walked into the living room and looked around in wonder.

"This is the first time I've been to your house," she said.

"Yeah, I was thinking about that, and I'm not sure why, other than we've been so busy with filming on location that we just hadn't made it here yet. But I've only been here a couple of days longer than you've been in your place."

She froze, and her eyes went wide as she hooked a thumb toward the foyer.

"Is there a doorbell cam?" she whispered.

"No." Logan laughed. "And if there was one, Dalton wouldn't have access to footage, since he's not paying the rent. You know, I really wouldn't care if he did."

Her eyes flashed, and he couldn't quite read her expression. For a moment, he wanted to backtrack, because he didn't want to scare her, but he had feelings for her and the only way this was going to work was if they were totally honest with each other.

He turned to face her. "Would it bother you if Dalton knew…about us?"

She opened her mouth to say something, then closed it and smiled, looking a little bewildered. "Are you saying you're ready to call us—" She motioned back and forth between the two of them. "Are we an *us*?"

He took her hands. "I know it's only been a few weeks since we met, but all I know is since that first day that you knocked on my sister's door, I haven't been able to stop thinking about you. You've been with me—right here—24-7." He tapped his heart.

Her hand fluttered to her own heart, but she didn't say anything. He put his hand over hers then brought it to his lips and kissed it as anticipation rushed through him.

She nodded. "I think we have something good here. Something really, really good."

He leaned down and kissed her, sweet and slow. For the first time in ages, life felt right. No, more than that… With her, life felt worth living.

"Are you going to show me around your place?" she asked.

After the quick tour, they ended up in the kitchen. He had selected a jazz playlist. The song "The Way You Look Tonight" played through the speakers as he poured her a glass of cava.

"To us." He raised his glass and touched it to hers.

"To us," she said.

They caught up on what had been happening while he'd been in Beaufort. Gabby had made it home safely. She only had good things to say about him. She and Sophie had recorded a scene on the beach with the B crew, but since there was no drama, it probably wouldn't make the cut. He and his brothers had secured the Beaufort listing.

"It was good to spend time with them," he said. "It was good bonding time. Maybe next week you and I can take a drive up there. The house is amazing, but it's in dire need of your touch."

"I am so here for it. Just let me know when."

When he took the crab legs out of the refrigerator to put them on to steam, she came up behind him and put her arms around him and kissed his neck.

"This is my favorite meal. Did I tell you that?"

He put the lid on the pot and turned around. Pulling her in close, he rested his forehead on hers. She had, but the words that spilled out on a shrug were "I guess we are just that connected."

By the time they finished dinner, he had a little buzz from the wine and was sticky from the crab and drawn butter.

He reached across the table and took her hand.

"I'm a mess. I really should wash my hands—"

"Me, too. I'm a mess. You're a mess. Let's be messy together."

She laughed, and it sounded like chimes striking just the right note to soothe his soul.

"I love that thought." She propped her elbow on the table, leaned her chin on her fist and gazed at him. The candles flickered. "Life…and love…can get so messy. God knows we've both dealt with more than our share of mess, but the best lesson I've learned is it's all in how you deal with it." She paused and sipped her cava. "I think I'm ready to deal with another person's messiness again. Are you sure you are, Logan?"

She arched a brow at him and blew him a kiss across the table. Then she excused herself to the bathroom, leaving him to sit with the question.

As Cassie walked away, he searched his soul.

It was one thing to say they were an *us*. Taking a woman to his bed was completely different than letting her into his life…or his heart.

He'd been with other women since Natalie, but they'd filled a need. He could never seem to thaw out enough to…care.

The gates opened, and thoughts of Natalie drifted into Logan's head—the good times and the times that could've been better. The *us* that they'd been hadn't gotten the chance to clean up the mess they'd made of their life together.

Logan went into the kitchen and stuck his hands under the faucet. He held his breath and waited for the inevitable onslaught of pain and self-loathing that always ambushed him when her ghost reminded him of how poorly he'd handled *that night*.

But was it her *ghost* taunting him? Or was it simply his own form of self-flagellation?

He let his mind—his heart—go somewhere he'd never gone until now. If Natalie had survived, would they have been able to get past her lies and betrayal? Because, yes, she had betrayed him by not telling him the truth. By not trusting him.

The question felt too big, but something else felt different this time.

If Bob and Lorraine could absolve him of their daughter's death—actually, never even hold him responsible—who was he to continue to hide from life, making a mess of his own future, living in limbo as he kept trying and retrying his case, pronouncing himself guilty every time?

As he stood there drying his hands, he acknowledged that he would never know how things would've turned out with Natalie. Their unresolved ending was tragic and horrible, but it didn't cancel out how much he'd loved her.

A new voice sounded up from the ashes of his soul: blaming himself wasn't going to change anything, and moving on with his life and learning from his mistakes was the best way to tidy up the mess of his first marriage.

He'd known that since his talk with Bob and Lorraine, since the night Cassie had told him he needed to give himself some grace and start living. But it had taken until now to let himself believe it.

He would always love Natalie. She was his first love.

But he knew that his late wife's better angel wouldn't want him to suffer for the rest of his life.

When Cassie returned, he was in the living room. He had put the half dozen key lime truffles on a plate and opened another bottle of cava.

"Come here," he said. "You have to taste this."

He picked up one of the truffles, and she bit into it.

"Oh my gosh, that's delicious. What is that? Key lime and chocolate?"

He nodded and popped the other half into his mouth. He handed her a glass of cava and clinked his glass to hers.

"It's great with the cava, isn't it?" he said.

"This chocolate is my new obsession. Don't tell me where you got these, because I will buy every single one."

As they shared another, the music switched over to Ella Fitzgerald's "I Got It Bad."

"Dance with me." She took his glass and set it down next to hers.

As he held her close and they swayed together, he could feel her heart pounding.

Or maybe it was his heart beating in time with hers.

Things had shifted tonight. What would it be like

to take his time getting to know the intricacies of her body? The peaks and valleys, the textures, the rhythms, what she liked and how she liked it? It was so personal. So intimate.

His body reacted.

Even though it wasn't the first time he'd been with a woman since losing Natalie, it was the first time that it had the potential to mean something.

That's why he didn't want to rush things.

When the song ended, he cradled her face in his palms and kissed her softly, gently. Her fingers found their way into his hair, pulling him close, closer until they were kissing with a need so furious it was all-consuming.

Maybe we're not rushing things...

She dusted his lips with kisses and trailed them down his throat. His body responded to the heady feel of her mouth on his skin.

She looked up at him with a sultry smile that teased him and had him longing to tell her that he wanted her in his bed...underneath him...on top of him...next to him. But her mouth reclaimed his, and he decided he would show her rather than talk about it.

It could've been minutes or hours...he had no idea—all knew was that he had to have her.

"Can you stay tonight?" he murmured.

"For a while. I'll need to go home and take care of Luna at some point."

He considered calling Sophie and asking her if she could go over and see to the dog, but he didn't want to break the spell.

"What if we stayed here for a while and then went to your place?" he asked.

"That sounds perfect. You can stay the night."

He smoothed a lock of hair off her forehead, kissed the skin he'd just uncovered, then searched her eyes. "Are you sure about this? Because if this is too soon for you, we can wait. It's important to me that you're completely honest about everything, especially about how you feel."

"You want me to be honest with you?" she asked, staring up at him.

He nodded.

"Honestly, I've never wanted anything more in my life. Not even those truffles."

He laughed softly and bit gently at her bottom lip, then kissed her again, long and slow, before leading her down the hallway to his bed.

In his bedroom, they stopped by the bed. His hands found hers, and he laced their fingers together. Their hands tarried a moment, gripping, flexing, hesitating... He was silently giving her one last chance to duck out if she wasn't ready for what was about to happen.

But she stayed.

He let go of her hands, and his arms closed around her. She tucked herself into him and buried her face in his chest. He breathed in the scent of her—that delicious smell of flowers and sunshine and spice. A scent that was so her it hit him in a place that nearly knocked him off his feet. Instead of coming undone, he took a deep breath and melted into her on a rush of red-hot need.

He claimed her mouth. His fingers slipped before sweeping down the outer edges of her body to claim her bottom.

Then, somehow, he'd tugged away her dress. She'd unbuttoned his jeans and soon they'd gotten rid of every barrier between them until they stood together naked and longing.

He eased her onto the bed. It was madness how much he needed her. Sheer, unmitigated madness.

They took their time exploring each other.

When he was sure she was ready, he took a condom from the drawer in his bedside table. She helped him roll it on, and he eased inside her. Starting with slow, gentle strokes that coaxed one moan after another from her, and building to fever pitch, their bodies went over the edge together, spasming and liquefying like wax in a flame.

Afterward, they lay together, sweaty and spent. Logan pulled her into his arms, and she tucked her body into him. As his senses settled back into place, he knew he was in deep. He would never let this woman go.

* * *

"Spoiler alert!" Sophie whispered to Cassie and Logan. She motioned for them to follow her into Cassie's backyard away from the crew, who were setting up to film a scene with Cassie and Logan making cookies for one of his open houses. "Word on the street has it that Dalton has new doorbell-cam footage."

Cassie glanced at Logan, and he looked at her. His brows shot up.

They'd gotten back to her house around midnight and taken Luna out, and then Logan had stayed until 6:00 a.m., when they'd remembered that they were scheduled to film in Cassie's kitchen at 10:00 a.m. Logan had taken care to park his truck out of the sight line of the doorbell camera. Last night, they'd entered through the garage—also out of camera range. This morning, Logan had left by the back door and had made a point of using the front door—and waving at the camera—when he'd arrived for work.

Had Dalton adjusted the camera's parameters?

Both of them looked back at Sophie, who had a knowing look on her face.

"Scared ya, didn't I? I have no idea if he has new footage, but I did overhear him talking to Chris, who handles edits, that he wants to trot out the doorbell-cam footage and splice it—or whatever they do to add footage—into one of the scenes. When he saw me listening, he stopped talking. He seems kind of jumpy, which makes me think he might have something else up his sleeve. Just beware.

"Also, if you want to keep y'all's private life private, you might want to be a little more discreet when you spend the night together. I saw your truck out there, and all it would take was one drive-by for Dalton to twig to what's going on. But good for you guys. I'm tickled pink that you two are together."

Yes, she did want to keep her private life private, but even the thought of Dalton interfering couldn't darken Cassie's mood.

Logan had been warm and loving both last night and this morning. Not a trace of lover's regret, which took Cassie's breath away. Last night had been even better than she'd hoped it would be. Logan had been gentle and sweet…oh, hell, who was she kidding? He had been hot and spicy, holding nothing back last night. It had been mind-blowing. Even remembering it made her lady parts wake up and sing the "Hallelujah" chorus.

Even so, in the light of day and faced with the real possibility of Dalton broadcasting their relationship across the nation, Cassie couldn't help but wonder if Logan would still not be bothered by Dalton knowing…*about us?*

She thought about the day when she'd locked herself out and Logan had come to her rescue. That was only a few weeks ago, but they'd both come so far. So very far.

On that very first day, it would've seemed like the end of the world for Dalton to broadcast footage of her wearing a dog-food bag, much less hold their newly minted relationship up for public scrutiny.

She let it roll around in her mind—her heart— for a moment, and she realized she didn't care who knew, or better yet, what anyone else thought.

"Bless his heart," Cassie said. "If he thinks embarrassing me will be good for ratings…go for it. If I don't get embarrassed over it, then it will be a big nothing."

"Right. You need to borrow a page from Cameron Diaz's character, Kimmy, in the movie *My Best Friend's Wedding*. Remember how Julia Roberts's character tried to humiliate Kimmy by manipulating her into singing karaoke? But, bad voice and all, she ended up being even more endearing."

The reference to *My Best Friend's Wedding* made Cassie remember Troy's phone call. Basking in these feelings for Logan, she knew that the opposite of love wasn't hate, it was feeling nothing. Tonight, she would tell Logan that Troy had called her. She'd planned on doing it last night, but with the way things had progressed, Troy had been the last person on her mind.

After all that talk about honesty and how important it was to him, she wanted to tell Logan because she loved him and she didn't want there to be any secrets between them.

"I can talk to Dalton about using the footage if you want," Logan said.

"You're my hero. You were my hero on that first day, and you still are now." Cassie leaned in and planted a kiss on his lips. Her arms closed around his neck.

"Okay, you two." Sophie pulled a face and pointedly looked away from Cassie and Logan. "I would tell you to get a room, but I'm afraid you might take me literally and go AWOL."

"Who had gone AWOL?" Dalton asked as he stepped outside, passing Sophie as she went in the house.

"My sense of humor," Logan said.

"Where'd your sense of humor go, Logie?" Dalton's voice was patronizing. "Do you need me to send a PA out to find it for you?"

"Look," Logan said. "There are rumbles that you're thinking about using the doorbell-cam footage, possibly taking it out of context. You need to know that's just not cool."

Dalton smiled. "I can assure you that I've never spent a single day in my life concerned about being cool."

"Maybe it would do you some good to think about other people's feelings for a change," he said. "There are other more important things than this ridiculous reality show."

Dalton's shit-eating grin morphed into a smirk. "I

realize you're defending your girlfriend's honor, but you both signed a contract. That contract clearly details that all footage shot can be used on the show at the discretion of the executive producer. That would be me. Why don't you just get in there and do your job like you're being paid to do?"

"The contract reads that we are each responsible for participating in fifteen scenes and after that we're free to go."

That's right…it was true. Cassie recalled the part of the contract, but she'd read it as more of an out clause, since there were monetary repercussions for cutting out early. Because of that, she had no intention of leaving until after the production crew had called an official wrap. Surely Logan wouldn't leave early. Especially not on her behalf.

She put her hand on his shoulder. "It's okay, Logan. Really. I'm sure it will all work out."

"No, it's not okay," Logan said. "Cassie, you've got to quit letting people walk all over you. Especially people who don't give a crap about anyone but themselves."

Logan turned and went back inside.

Dalton walked in the opposite direction and disappeared around the side of her house.

Cassie stood there alone, reeling like she'd just been slapped in the face. She tried to tell herself that Logan hadn't meant that the way she was taking it—as a dig. But she'd poured out her heart to him about how her ex-in-laws had treated her poorly and had never accepted her after she'd bent over backward to make them see that she was a good person and a good wife to their son.

Maybe she was being overly sensitive, but it sure felt like Logan had poked at a bruise that hadn't had a chance to heal. It made no sense that he would turn things around on her.

Unless…unless Sophie's joking around about them spending the night together had hit Logan's own tender spot. Maybe he wasn't as ready to go public with all the *us and we* business as he'd claimed last night.

A lightning bolt of panic coursed through her as she feared that, just like her in-laws, Logan had decided she wasn't good enough. The stink associated with her being the daughter of a convicted con man might rub off on him and his. Were her father's bad choices and squalid reputation ruining things again?

Cassie felt herself sinking, but in a flash she reminded herself that she'd never told Logan about her father.

Now, she never would.

"Cassie, we're ready to get started," Zoe called from the back door. "We need you in the kitchen."

Cassie shored herself up. She hadn't asked Logan to fight this battle over the doorbell-cam footage for her. If he was going to step in anyway and then throw barbs about her not standing up for herself, this would be a good place to show that she wasn't going to let people walk on her.

In the kitchen, before she could say a word to Logan, he took her hand and walked her toward the pantry, the only place in the small kitchen where they might have any privacy—though he kept his hand laced through hers. They hadn't yet put their microphones on, but Logan didn't seem too worried about being private.

"I'm sorry about what happened out there," Logan whispered. His back was to the crew, and the cameras weren't rolling yet. "Dalton provoked me, and that was all for him and not supposed to be directed toward you. I hope you'll forgive me."

Relief rushed through her. She hated that Logan still had a problem with Dalton, but she was happy she and Logan were good. That he wasn't having second thoughts.

"To me it's important when a person makes a heartfelt apology. Thank you for that. As far as I'm concerned, it never happened."

Logan gave her a hand a squeeze and then leaned in and dusted her lips with a kiss. Cassie braced herself for Dalton to pop up from out of nowhere and make a spectacle out of it, but when they turned and went back to the counter where the ingredients and equipment to make Cassie's famous peanut butter cookies were laid out, Dalton was nowhere to be seen and the rest of the crew was busy going over notes and getting ready to shoot.

Logan and Cassie smiled at each other. They were keeping a secret right in front of everyone, and there was something very sexy about it.

A few minutes later, after they put their microphones on, Dalton called everyone to order, and the cameras began rolling. Dalton was acting like himself, and maybe even being a little less director-like than usual, because he was letting Cassie and Logan talk as they made cookies together. It was more like Cassie made the cookies and Logan sampled the dough and explained the house in Beaufort and his thoughts on staging it.

"The house is stunning," he said. "It was built in the early nineteenth century, and it has a lot of historical significance, including some pirate lore, associated with it."

Before he could start talking like a pirate, someone knocked on the door, and it pulled Cassie out of the scene.

"Cut," Dalton said.

Her gaze snapped to the producer/director, and she expected him to pitch a fit over the interruption. One of the PAs would surely pay, because someone was always stationed at points where onlookers might be tempted to interrupt. Cassie's money was on a curious neighbor seeing the production trucks on the street and wanting the inside scoop.

Instead, Dalton smiled.

"We have a little twist for you today. There's a special guest. So, Cassie, I need for you to walk in and answer the door after we start rolling."

Her heart leaped. What if Dalton had decided to bring Gabby back as a full-time cast member? Her sister was the one who'd always dreamed of acting. *Ohhh*, she could move into the second bedroom. It would be such fun. It had to be. She couldn't think of anyone else Dalton would bring in this late in the game.

Cassie smiled and tried to tamp down her excitement as the cameras started rolling and she walked toward the front door.

When she opened the door, she blinked and frowned, because she didn't recognize the tall, gaunt man standing on her porch, clasping a hat in his hands in front of him. Unsure of what to do, she glanced at Ernie, the second cameraman, who was standing just behind the guy.

"Cassie?" The stranger's voice cracked, and he cleared his throat. "Cassie, don't you recognize me? I'm your father."

Chapter Fourteen

Cassie shut the door in the man's face.

I don't have a father.

She stared at the closed door, feeling like her knees were about to buckle. This wasn't happening. This couldn't be happening. Then she remembered Gabby's warning, that she should be prepared, because when Ray had contacted her, he'd sounded determined to find Cassie.

But how did it happen? If he'd found her on his own, why was he part of the filming? Clearly, Dalton's fingerprints were all over this. He'd said they had a little twist, a *surprise guest* for today's filming.

"Stop filming," Cassie said, still facing the door. "Who brought this man here?"

She whirled around and saw Logan standing a few feet behind her.

"Who was that?" he asked.

Gerry, the first cameraman, stepped closer, recording the exchange between Cassie and Logan.

One of Dalton's cardinal rules was that the cast was to ignore the camera during filming. If, heaven forbid, they acknowledged it in any way, the scene couldn't be used since he was going for a seamless, unscripted appearance, even though everything was painstakingly staged.

It was all so phony.

"I said, stop filming," Cassie yelled. Several of the crew startled and moved back out of her way as she walked up to Gerry and put her hand over the lens.

"Cut," Dalton called.

"You're damn right," Cassie answered. "You'd better cut and explain to me why you brought that man here, Dalton."

Dalton's lips twisted into a smirk, and Cassie decided she didn't want to know.

"Never mind," she said. "I don't care how you found him. You have crossed the line, Dalton. Everybody get out of my house, please. I'm serious, everyone. Out. Now."

"Excuse me?" Dalton laughed. "Top Drawer Productions is paying for this rental. We don't have to go anywhere."

"Then I will." Cassie pushed past Gerry and the PA and Dalton and left through the back door.

Leaving through the back door... Wasn't that the story of her life? How many times had she been forced to leave in shame through the back door because of her father, the con man? She inhaled a ragged breath, and that was when she realized tears were streaming down her face.

"Cassie, wait," Logan called.

She stopped. A mélange of relief and dread washed through her. Logan wasn't letting her walk away, but how was she going to explain this to him?

"Who was that?" he asked when he caught up with her. "Who was that man?"

She was paralyzed. She couldn't speak. She could barely breathe.

"I thought I heard him say he was your father, but that's impossible, because you told me your father is dead."

She closed her eyes and stood there until she found her voice.

"I haven't seen that man in twenty-one years, since the police dragged him out of the house in handcuffs in front of Gabby and me. I was only six years old."

"So, what are you saying? Your father's alive? You told me he was dead."

The look on his face cut her to the core.

"I said that because my father was sentenced to

thirty years in prison for conning people. I didn't even know that he'd been released from jail until Gabby told me when she was here."

Logan squinted at her as if he couldn't comprehend what she was saying.

"So, you lied to me." His voice was flat.

"Not really. Ray Davis is dead to me. He never paid a cent of child support. He drove my mother to an early grave."

"Why couldn't you just tell me the truth?"

"I did tell you the truth. I told you *my* truth. That man in there is dead to me."

The look Logan gave her broke her heart.

"Okay, Logan. You want the truth? At the first meeting I said both of my parents were gone. Since my mom is dead, I know it seemed like my dad had passed away, too. Then when you opened up about Natalie deceiving you, I didn't know how to backtrack to clarify that my dad was alive, that he was in jail. It felt like it would've reopened wounds – for both of us. Now, you think I lied to you.

In my experience, after I've told people my father is a felon, opinions change. You know, like grifting is in the gene pool, and I'll rip them off, just like my old man. Do you have any idea what it's like for someone to judge you—to marginalize you—because of the sins of your father? Of course you don't—your father is hardworking. He's a good man. You have a good family, Logan. That's all I've ever wanted, but because of him, it's always out of my reach."

Logan stared at her. His expression was inscrutable.

"Like I said a while ago, if that's how the people in your life have treated you, you need new friends. Why didn't you trust me, Cassie?"

"Because I was afraid of exactly this kind of reaction."

"This reaction is not because of who your father is or what he's done. It's because you lied to me after knowing that's one thing I can't deal with. It makes me wonder what else you might be hiding."

"That's not fair, Logan."

When he didn't answer, she closed her eyes and drew in a deep breath through her nose, trying to dilute the humiliation she was feeling, trying to think of a way to fix this. Logan had been in a funky mood since he'd gotten back this morning. Maybe he'd changed his mind.

"Are you just looking for a way out, Logan? Did last night scare you and now you're using this as a get-out-of-jail-free card?" She realized the irony of her words and bit down on her bottom lip.

"Don't turn this around on me, Cassie. I fell in love with you. I would've never— I would've understood if you would've trusted me."

He fell in love with me?

She swallowed hard. "You don't love me if you can just walk away like this."

Logan shook his head. "I have to go."

He turned and walked off, leaving Cassie standing outside alone. She needed to get out of there, too. When she looked up, she saw Gerry aiming the camera at her.

Her car was in the garage—and her keys were in the house. She thought about going next door to Sophie's house, but that was a bad idea. Sophie would take her brother's side.

She'd become so fond of the McFaddens that they'd started to feel like the family she'd always wanted, but Cassie would have to let them go. They would rally around their son, because blood was always thicker than water.

The only thing she could do was set off on foot. She walked for a long time, until she finally found herself on Main Street. Keeping her head down, she swiped away tears as she walked past the Sandcastle Real Estate office, past all the quaint little shops and the restaurant where she, Gabby and Sophie had had so much fun filming their lunch scene. The conversation might have been semiscripted, but the fun and closeness had been real.

She stopped in the park where they'd announced *Selling Sandcastle* to the public and sat on a bench.

It all seemed like it had happened a long time ago, or maybe even to someone else. Because no matter where she ran or whom she pretended to be—or not to be—it would always come back to the fact that she was the daughter of a man who cheated people out of their hard-earned money.

She may have kept Troy's last name after they divorced, but that didn't change the fact that she was still Cassie Davis, the daughter of a con artist. When it came down to it, wasn't she a con herself for pretending to be someone she wasn't?

The sun had shifted in the sky, and she realized she'd been gone awhile. Since she and Logan had both walked off the set—and away from each other—the crew had probably cleared out. She'd left Luna in her kennel in the bedroom. The poor girl would need to go out.

As she retraced her steps, Cassie decided she would go back to the house, take care of Luna and prepare to go back to Orlando. Of course, she'd need to talk to Bert. Since he'd hired her as an in-house stager, she owed him the courtesy of a resignation… and an explanation. His clients wouldn't want a grifter's daughter in their houses.

As Cassie turned on to North Ridge Court, she had a straight shot down the street and could see that the film crew's trucks were gone.

She hoped that the crew had had the decency to lock up the place. Not that Tinsley Cove was a crime haven.

In the next beat, she also realized that if the crew

did lock the doors, she'd be locked out of the house again.

Like that first day, things had come full circle. Proof that it was time for her to go.

As she drew closer, she could make out that some-one was sitting on her front porch step.

A man.

Her heart leaped at the thought that Logan might be waiting for her, but as she got closer she realized it wasn't Logan. It was her father sitting there.

He saw her and waved like he was flagging down an old friend. It was too late to turn around and walk away.

Without preamble, she walked past him onto the porch and said, "Why are you here? Why now, after all these years?"

He looked her straight in the eyes. "Because I want to make amends. If you'll just give me a chance."

"You haven't been a part of my life for twenty-one years. You didn't even bother to write. What makes you think you can just waltz back into my life now? For that matter, how did you find me?"

She was certain that Gabby hadn't told him. If he'd paid her a visit and she'd inadvertently let it slip, Gabby would've called her to give her the heads-up. The same way Gabby had forewarned Cassie about Troy's engagement and that their dad been in touch with her.

"That producer of yours found me," Ray said. "He said he stumbled across my name when he'd run a background check on you."

A background check?

Cassie did not recall giving permission for Dalton to do a background check.

"Before I forget," Ray said. "Your neighbor dropped this off for you."

He nodded toward Sophie's house as he handed her an envelope.

Heart pounding at the possibility of it being a note from Logan, Cassie tore open the envelope, which contained a note and a key.

Dear Cassie,
I was worried that you might've left without your keys. Here's a spare, just in case. I took Luna out to do her business, so she should be comfortable until you get back.

I'll be away filming with a client who is looking for a rental, and I'm not sure when I'll get home. I don't know what happened because Logan won't tell me anything, but if you want to talk when I get back from filming, I'm here. Talk soon.
Hugs,
Sophie

That's so nice.

Tears welled in Cassie's eyes, and her breath hitched.

That was one of the things she would miss most about Tinsley Cove—people looking out for people rather than it being every person left to fend for herself. Since the divorce, Gabby was the only person in the world she'd let herself trust.

Maybe Logan was right. Other than Gabby, maybe she had surrounded herself with the wrong people. Or maybe that's the type of person she attracted by closing herself off and not letting people know the real her.

She felt Ray watching her and looked up.

"Thank you for delivering this." She held up Sophie's note. "I need to go. Take care."

As she started to put the key in the door, Ray said, "Cassie, please give me a chance. You, Gabriella and I are family. You're my daughters. We are all we have."

"I haven't seen you or heard from you since I was six years old. It's been twenty-one years, Ray. I don't even know you. You have no right to burst back into my life after all these years and expect for us to be a family…to pick up like nothing was wrong."

At first, Cassie thought Ray was hanging his head, but then she realized he was digging in the messenger bag that was slung across his body.

"Will you please hear me out?" he asked as he continued to dig in the bag.

"No," Cassie said. "I don't want to hear what you have to say. You had more than two decades to say it, but you chose not to be part of my life."

It hit her that it would've been a better choice to tell people that she and her father were estranged. But she'd gotten so used to thinking of him as dead that it had become a part of who she was.

"You may have been in prison, but you have no idea what it was like to be left behind to clean up the mess you made. It was its own particular brand of hell, Ray."

He pulled a thick stack of letters bound with a rubber band from his bag and handed them to her.

"Cassie, I tried to keep in touch, but every letter I wrote was returned to me."

She stared at the bundle as if he were offering her a box of coral snakes.

"Please, take them." His hand with the letters inched closer.

Curious, she took them and glanced at the top letter on the stack. In looping red script—that looked suspiciously like her mother's hand—were the words *return to sender*.

The letter on top was postmarked a few months after the feds had burst in and taken him away.

"I don't expect you to welcome me with open arms, but I do hope you will read the letters and see that I tried. I'm not blaming your mother. She was only trying to protect you. I left her—and you girls—in a bad way. But I never stopped loving you or hoping that one day I would get the chance to make it up to you."

He started to walk away, but he stopped and turned back. "The only reason I agreed to Dalton's stunt was because it gave me the chance to see you. I needed to know that you're okay."

But can't you see I'm not okay?

"You're more than okay, Cassie. You're a force. A survivor. Even so, I can see how much this has upset you. So I will withdraw from the show. There was no contract, just a verbal agreement to film one episode. It'll be easy enough to cancel, because I'm not sure they got any footage they can use and I'm heading back to Florida today."

She thought about asking him where in Florida he would be, but the words stayed lodged in her throat as she stood on the porch watching him walk away.

As she unlocked the door, the doorbell cam caught her eye. She didn't bristle. Instead, she resigned herself to let Dalton do whatever he wanted with the footage. It would be her parting gift to him, since she was leaving early.

A pang of regret ricocheted through her. It had been fun and exciting to be part of a television show, but it had also come with some unexpected down sides. At the top of that list was how Dalton had been a lot more cutthroat than she'd expected.

For a moment, she pondered whether being surprised by this side of him meant she was a bad judge of character… What had it meant that she'd believed Logan when he'd said he was falling in love with her?

Was she the eternal optimist, always wanting to see the best in people, or was she simply blind?

No matter what, it was probably good that she was moving on and away from people who treated her poorly.

People?

Dalton was one person. The rest of the people she'd met in Tinsley Cove had been lovely. That's how she would remember them.

Especially Logan. Her heart ached at the thought of losing him. She loved him, but how could she lose him when she'd never really had him?

She would remember him and this show as an adventure.

And Ray…her father. She had no idea what to think about him. He'd seemed so earnest. He hadn't asked her for anything, but Cassie couldn't help but wonder when the other shoe would fall. He was a con man, after all.

Once inside, she'd set the stack of letters on the dining room table. After loving on Luna for a bit, Cassie turned her attention to organizing for her move back to Orlando. She hadn't been at it for more than an hour when there was another knock at her door.

She worried it might be Ray, and thought about

not answering, but what if it was Logan coming over to talk things out?

She was wrong on both accounts. It was Dalton and Bert.

At least she wouldn't have to go into the office to tell him she was going back to Orlando, but if they'd come to tag-team her, trying to talk her into redoing the scene with Ray, they had another think coming.

However, once everyone was settled in the living room, she noticed that Dalton seemed oddly subdued.

"Y'all didn't have to come all the way over here," she said. "But since you're here, I have a couple of things to say, and I'd like to go first."

The men nodded.

"First, Dalton, you were way out of line bringing Ray here. Just because I agreed to be on the show, it doesn't mean you have carte blanche to every aspect of my life."

She stopped there, hoping the point would hit home.

Still, she braced herself for him to start in on how scenes like that were off-the-charts good drama. Reality TV gold. Great for the show.

Instead, Dalton surprised her. "In retrospect, I realize that was a bridge too far."

"After I heard about what happened this morning," Bert said, "Dalton and I had a come-to-Jesus meeting. We've established some parameters for the show. He agrees that not only does he not have free rein, but that having no guardrails isn't necessarily good for the show. Especially if it means losing good cast members, like you, Cassie."

"We both have come to ask you to stay," Dalton said. "With some adjustments made, of course."

Dalton looked her in the eyes for the first time since he'd arrived. Maybe she was looking for the best in him, but she thought he seemed sincere.

"I don't know," Cassie said. "I guess one thing I've learned after being on this show is that I'm not sure if I want my life to be an open book. I know I should've considered that before I agreed to be a cast member, but I haven't had any contact with my father for more than two decades. The father I knew then has been essentially dead to me for most of my cognizant life. Do you know what it was like to have you conjure him up and present him to me on television?"

She considered telling him she knew that he had asked Gabby to blindside her with the news about Troy, but she was just too emotionally exhausted.

"I get that," Dalton said.

"That's why Dalton has agreed there will be no more personal surprises," Bert said. "Anything like that will be agreed to in advance. Would that make you feel better about staying on?"

Cassie shrugged. "It sounds good, but I would need Dalton to put it in writing so that there are no misunderstandings."

"I'm sure we can come to a meeting of the minds," Dalton said. "As long as you understand we can't exclude something like your and Logan's relationship."

"What relationship?" Bert asked.

"Come on, Papa Bear, where have you been?" Dalton said. "It's right in front of everyone's face. Cassie and Logan are a thing."

Dalton's words cut Cassie deeply.

"No, Dalton, we are not a thing," she said. "Bert, you don't have to worry about your son falling for the daughter of a felon."

Bert knitted his brow, and Cassie waited for him to backpedal.

"Cassie, you are not your father," Bert said. "If you and my son are a *thing*, as Dalton put it, that's your business. Not mine. All I want for Logan is for him to be happy. What is my business is, is that you've clearly got a talent for design. It would be a huge loss for Sandcastle Real Estate to lose you. Regardless of what you do about the show, I hope you will seriously consider staying in Tinsley Cove and continuing your fantastic work."

Her head was spinning. She told Dalton and Bert that she would consider everything and let them know in the morning.

The McFaddens were not anything like Troy's family. It was clear that Bert had been oblivious to the relationship that had been blossoming between Logan and her. Would he and Bunny feel differently once they learned that Logan was furious with her? That he wanted nothing to do with her?

She had fallen hard for Logan, but clearly he wasn't ready for where they'd been headed. Yesterday he'd said he'd fallen in love with her, but today he'd changed his mind.

Maybe it would be best for her to take some time and space to get over him.

Maybe it would be best to go back to Orlando and start over.

Chapter Fifteen

"Hello? Is anybody home?"

Logan was sitting on the screened back porch drinking a beer when he heard his mom call out from the kitchen.

"Out here," he said.

"What are you doing out here in the dark all alone?" Bunny asked. "I knocked, but no one answered. The door was unlocked, so I let myself in. I made a big pot of chili and a pan of corn bread this afternoon. I thought Cassie might be here, so I brought over enough for two."

"Cassie's not here," he said and took a draw on his beer.

"Well, that's a shame," Bunny said. "Actually, I

brought over enough for six. So even if you have a bowl tonight, there will be plenty to share with her another time."

This was Bunny's not-so-subtle way of fishing for information. Sneak attack through food.

Actually, he was kind of hungry.

"I'm going to fix myself a bowl," he said. "Care to join me?"

"Oh, no, I'm stuffed, sweetie, but you go ahead. I'll sit with you while you eat."

The chili was still warm. As Logan dished up a good helping, he wondered what Cassie was eating for dinner. He shouldn't care, but it was just an idle thought.

Maybe she'd invited her father to dinner. Good for her if she did.

That wasn't what was bothering him. The fact that she'd lied. She didn't trust him, that's what was burning a hole in his gut. It felt like such a betrayal. Especially after he'd opened up to her about everything he'd gone through with Natalie.

Bunny sipped the cup of Earl Grey she'd made herself, and they sat together in silence for a few bites as Logan ate the chili.

"Can I talk to you about something that's been on my mind?" Bunny asked.

Logan shrugged. "Sure."

"I have been so happy to have you home," she said. "You know nothing warms my heart like having all four of my babies within a ten-mile radius. But what breaks my heart is to know that one of you is unhappy. You, my love, haven't seemed happy since you came home." She held up her hand. "Actually, let me amend that, because it's not exactly true. A few days ago, you seemed more like yourself than you have in a long time…"

She trailed off, and Logan knew she was talking about the time before Natalie died, but neither of them filled in that detail.

"Your father mentioned that you walked off the set today when you were filming at Cassie's house. Do you want to talk about it?"

Logan took his time chewing and swallowing the bite in his mouth.

"There's nothing much to say."

He took a long draw of his beer.

"I'll cut to the chase," Bunny said. "I know that you agreed to come home and take part in this crazy reality show for me. I can see that you're not really having a good time doing it. Logan, you don't have to do this for me. You need to live your own life. Whether that's here or back in California, it's your choice. Although I would like to go on record and register my vote for you to move back to Tinsley Cove permanently."

She smiled and winked at him. Logan knew that was her way of saying she was only half joking.

"I do have some good news that may make it a

little bit easier for you to decide what's best for you. I got the results back from my tests, and the doctor says I am officially cancer-free."

"That is wonderful news, Mom." Logan stood up and hugged his mom. There was nothing like that to put things into perspective. "Why did you cook tonight? Why aren't we taking you out to dinner to celebrate?"

She smiled and waved him off. "I'll take you up on that another night. I thought it was important for you to know that my health does not need to factor into your decision. You never know how these things are going to go." She shrugged, and for a moment the worry he'd seen when she'd first been diagnosed flashed in her eyes, but it disappeared just as quickly. "Logan, I can't begin to express how much I appreciate you indulging me by coming home and being part of *Selling Sandcastle*. If you're not having a good time, you don't have to continue."

He thought about it for a moment, weighing his words. He wasn't enjoying it, but being back in Tinsley Cove hadn't been so bad.

"I don't know that I'm cut out for television of any kind, but I'm not minding the real estate gig. It's surprising, because I always felt this need to do something different. You know, make my own way apart from the family business, but that may have been a mistake. Or, who knows, maybe I had to move to California and give general contracting a go before I could fully appreciate working with my family. Everything has its challenges. It just depends on how much it means to you."

Cassie flashed into his mind. She was the first person since Natalie who had meant something to him. Despite everything that had happened today, she was still special.

He'd spent a lot of time thinking about her today. He'd tried to put himself in her place. Tried to dissect the lie about her father—why she'd felt like she had to misrepresent Ray, why she couldn't confide in him. But what had Logan done to earn her trust? Especially after turning away from her when things got messy.

Still, lies were a trigger for him. When a person misrepresented herself, he couldn't help but wonder what else she might be hiding. And he knew that was totally unfair. Maybe he was lying to himself by not giving her the opportunity to fully explain.

Maybe she was right… Maybe he was looking for a way out. Now, after sitting alone for the better part of the day, he wasn't so sure he wanted out.

"Is that your way of saying you might join the business?" Bunny asked, not even trying to hide the hope in her eyes.

"I certainly don't have anything waiting for me back in California."

Over the years, he'd sold most of his belongings, only keeping the bare basics—a bed, a chair, a table.

A friend's wife had shown him how to sell Natalie's coveted designer clothes through various outlets online that dealt in high-end apparel.

Logan was both amazed and appalled at the prices secondhand clothes and accessories commanded. Even so, the proceeds barely made a dent in the debt he owed for her overspending and medical bills.

It did give him some insight about why Natalie had felt such pressure to be dressed to the nines all the time and present such a perfect facade on her social media. Living in California hadn't helped.

The good news was he'd been paying down the debt for a while now. Between his real estate commissions and the money he'd make from the show, he would be debt-free in a matter of weeks. Especially once the house he listed in Beaufort sold.

"I know I've asked a lot already," Bunny said. "But I'm going to ask one more favor. Now that Cassie is going back to Orlando, Dalton is going to need all hands on deck. Could you stay with the show just a little bit longer until he comes up with an alternate plan?"

Logan did a double take.

"Who said Cassie was going back to Orlando? Did she say that?"

His mother nodded sadly. "Well, at least that's what your father told me. After the big hullabaloo that happened on the set today, he and Dalton went to talk to her, but she was pretty upset. I guess Dalton really overstepped his bounds this time. Her family challenges are nobody's business but her own. Obviously, she hasn't had a relationship with her father, and who does Dalton think he is to pull this man out of the woodwork and spring him on her like that? I can't say I blame her for wanting to go, though we are going to miss her desperately."

Logan felt like he had been kicked in the gut—and he deserved it. His mom was right. Cassie's family issues were private. He hadn't realized it until this moment, but it was similar to how he didn't like sharing what had happened with Natalie and the business he'd lost. Maybe if he'd been willing to show her a little more grace, she would've felt comfortable sharing with him.

Bunny tapped on her phone and pulled up her calendar.

"Let's see, today is the twenty-ninth…" Her voice trailed off as she calculated how many days of filming they had left.

Logan's heart lodged in his throat. It couldn't be the twenty-ninth.

"We need to have the Beaufort house staged by the fifth," Bunny said. "I wonder if we could talk Cassie into staying long enough to do that? She could stay with us at the house if Dalton decides to be a jackass and makes her leave the bungalow." She shrugged. "I suppose it's his prerogative since he's paying the rent. But we'll cross that bridge when we come to it."

"Today's not the twenty-ninth," Logan said. "It's the twenty-sixth."

"No, sweetie, see, today is the twenty-ninth." Bunny held her phone so he could see the date on her phone's lock screen. "You lost some days somewhere."

For a moment, the world went white and fuzzy around Logan before everything snapped back into focus.

Now it made sense why he had been in such a funk today. Today was the fifth anniversary of when they'd taken Natalie off life support. Logan had been so wrapped up in his own misery that he hadn't even realized today was the day. Even if his brain hadn't registered it, somehow his heart had intrinsically sensed it. Hence, his funk.

The worst part was that he had taken out his sadness and guilt on Cassie. How could he be so careless? Hadn't Natalie's death taught him that you don't always get the luxury of a second chance?

He was about to lose her on the anniversary of losing his wife.

It was only 7:00 p.m. He needed to acknowledge the day to Bob and Lorraine. Then he needed to go see Cassie.

He had a lot of mending to do and a very short window of time to do it in.

* * *

As Cassie sat on her bedroom floor folding and organizing her clothes in preparation for her move, she kept replaying in her head Bert McFadden saying she had a talent for design.

*I have talent.*her She'd made it her mantra.

Every time she pictured Logan walking away, she pushed the mental play button and soaked up Bert's compliment.

Why did it take someone else believing in her before she could believe in herself?

That would stop right now. Even though she wasn't continuing with the show, as soon as it aired, it would be the best design portfolio she could offer. In the meantime, she would print out the photos she'd taken of the rooms she'd staged and use those to get work.

Then she would concentrate on parlaying the exposure she'd get from *Selling Sandcastle* into starting her own business.

She had possibilities. That meant she needed to use this time to stand on her own two feet.

She told herself that, someday, she would meet the man she was supposed to be with and have the family she'd always wanted. If she never did, she'd found something she loved to do—designing rooms that made people feel like they'd come home.

It would just take time for the big Logan-size hole in her heart to heal.

Luna seemed to sense Cassie's sadness and plopped down next to where she was folding sweaters to pack away when she got the boxes tomorrow. The little dog leaning all her weight on her was like the best kind of tourniquet to stop the pain. Cassie scratched her best buddy behind her velvety ears.

Then, suddenly, Luna jumped up and started barking as she ran to the front door.

Cassie glanced at the clock on the nightstand. It was 8:30 p.m. Was someone here? She hadn't heard the doorbell or a knock.

Then she heard it.

Please don't let it be Ray coming back to pressure me into giving him a place to stay for the night.

Just in case, she got up, opened the plantation shutter on her bedroom window and peeked out at the driveway.

Her heart stopped then skipped into double time. It was Logan's truck. He was at her door. She should've known it was him by the way Luna sensed him and ran even before he'd had a chance to knock.

She looked in the mirror and fluffed up her hair and started to pinch some color into her cheeks but then stopped. Maybe he was here to be Dalton's messenger and evict her. She snorted at the ridiculous thought. Logan might be mad at her, but he wasn't mean.

Besides, she hadn't yet delivered the definitive

news to Dalton that she was leaving. That was first on the list for tomorrow.

As she made her way to the door, she forced herself to stop imagining why Logan was here. Mostly so she wouldn't get her hopes up that he'd come to talk things out. She couldn't deal with another crushing disappointment if he was here to, say, check the AC or disable the doorbell cam. Hmm…that could be the reason, since he was at the front door.

"Okay, Luna, stay back. Sit," she said as she put her hand on the knob. She took a deep breath, smiled to cover her nerves and opened the door.

"Hello," she said as her little dog bolted past her and right into Logan. He bent down and caught her with one arm. Of course. Luna loved him so much that she seemed to strategically launch herself right into his arms every time he was around.

Cassie totally understood. On more than one occasion, it had taken every fiber of self-control to stop herself from doing exactly the same thing.

Like right now.

But she needed to get used to the reality that she would never be in Logan's arms again.

Logan stood up and shepherded the dog back into the house. That's when Cassie realized that he'd been holding one arm behind his back this whole time.

As she shut the door, he presented her the most beautiful bouquet of pink peonies she'd ever seen.

"You said they were your favorites."

She accepted them and buried her face in them.

"You remembered."

"I don't expect flowers to excuse me for acting like such a jerk this morning, but I was hoping that you would show me enough grace to hear me out."

Grace. She smiled to herself. He was borrowing her word. He remembered that, too.

"That depends," she said.

"Sure. Anything you want."

"Are you willing to show yourself the same grace?"

She saw the tension in his face melt away, replaced by a heartrending frown.

"I am sorry about the way I acted today," he said. "It's your decision to tell me or not tell me about your father, when and if you're ready. In all fairness, I have a confession to make. I've kept my own secret. I've painted a false picture of myself because I wanted you to love me."

He stopped and stared into the middle distance, seeming to weigh his words.

Cassie's heart thudded as she waited. She gulped down a breath to stay quiet. Now was the time to listen, not fill the silence.

"A while ago you asked me what happened to my business."

She nodded.

He told her how he'd shut down and shut everyone out after losing Natalie. He'd let everything go.

He'd lost their house, lost his business. Basically, he'd lost his will to live.

"For the first few years, I would've been happier if they'd put me in the ground right beside her. I blamed myself, but now it seems like it was a copout."

"Hey," Cassie soothed. "That's not fair. You were devastated. You needed time to put everything back together."

"Yeah, but what kind of a loser just lets everything go to hell?"

"Remember, give yourself some grace. You didn't hurt anyone but yourself."

His face darkened, and he started to say something, but he stopped.

Cassie knew he was going to say he'd hurt Natalie. But he didn't. Instead, he stood there for a moment, staring at the ground until his face transformed.

"Knowing I destroyed my life make you think differently about me?" he asked.

"Does knowing my father conned innocent people out of their hard-earned savings make you look at me different?" she countered.

"No way." He didn't miss a beat.

"I don't think or feel differently about you, either. We can't define ourselves by our past mistakes, because we've both learned from them. We have to trust ourselves to do better, and we have to trust each other."

He took the flowers from her and opened his

arms. She melted into the sanctuary of Logan. *Her Logan.*

A few minutes later, Logan said, "Not to deflect, but Dalton was a total jackass for bringing your father here without telling you first. I thought my family was going to take him out, because they love you. As far as they're concerned, nobody messes with Cassie. Especially me. Still, given how I acted, maybe our jackassery levels are equal."

They laughed, and he pulled her close again.

"Cassie, I had no right to treat you that way, and if you will forgive me, I promise I will never do anything like that again."

He then told her that today was the fifth anniversary of Natalie's death and confessed that he hadn't realized today was the twenty-ninth until he'd been discussing logistics with his mother. He told her that he'd taken flowers to Natalie's parents, and they'd talked for a while.

"All day long, I thought today was the twenty-sixth, but somehow, my heart knew better," he said. "This is not an excuse, but I think that played a part in why I was in such a bad place this morning."

She didn't quite know what to say about this being the significant anniversary that she knew he'd been dreading, but listening felt like the right thing to do.

They sat down in the living room, and he told her about his visit with Bob and Lorraine.

"Essentially, they reinforced that it was time for

me to move on," he said. "It's really weird, but now, I feel like whatever was holding me back from living has finally released me. I feel free. That has everything to do with you."

His words took her breath away.

"The other night—jeez—was it just last night?" she pondered. "Anyway, it was when we were talking about life getting and being messy. That part is a given, but it's all in how you clean up the mess. All in how you decide to stage your life. Okay, that's kind of corny, isn't it? But I've been sulking around here all night thinking about how I was going to miss out on staging the Beaufort house. And, full disclosure—because I promise I will never keep anything from you again—that's not the only reason I was sulking. The main reason was because I was missing you, Logan. I thought I'd blown it and I— And I am talking too much. See, I told you I always do this when I get nervous."

He bent down and covered her mouth with his and kissed her gentle and slow, but like he meant it.

"There is no need for you to be nervous about anything anymore," he said. "I love you, Cassie. I know we haven't been together that long, but will you please consider staying in Tinsley Cove? Orlando is kind of a haul from here. But if going back to Orlando is important to you, I'll make it work on my end. Because I really want this—you and me—

to work. I need you in my life. Plus, my family has already adopted you."

She put her arms around his neck. "Yes, I'll stay, because I love you, Logan."

They kissed again.

"Plus," she said, "Luna would never forgive me if I took her away from you."

Epilogue

October

The entire population of Tinsley Cove gathered in Springdale Park for the premiere of *Selling Sandcastle*.

Sheila Larson, the president of the chamber of commerce, and her team had decorated the area like a Hollywood movie premiere, complete with movie lights, a red carpet, a jumbo screen on which the show would be projected and free popcorn for everyone.

Dressed in her gold beaded gown, Cassie was giddy with nerves, but the sight of Logan looking handsome in his tux helped ground her.

She, Logan and the rest of the McFadden family

would see the pilot episode for the first time right along with their friends and neighbors. Even though Dalton had agreed the doorbell-cam footage was off-limits, Cassie wondered, now that season one was in the can, if he might pull some kind of spectacle out of his sleeve to increase publicity. She wouldn't put it past him.

Gabby had their father had flown up for the festivities.

Yes, their father. It had taken a while for Cassie to summon the nerve, but she'd finally read the stack of letters he'd written to her while he was in prison. They told the story of a contrite man who had made many bad decisions and paid dearly for them. He'd only been twenty-five when he'd gone to jail. In many ways, he'd been a kid who had been struggling to support his family. He'd fallen in with a bad bunch who had lured him in with the promise of big, easy money.

Some of the things Cassie learned reading the letters and the subsequent dialogue that had started because of them was that he had tried to pay child support with the little money he earned doing jobs and taking classes, but Cassie's mother had refused it. In the only letter she'd written to him, she told him she wanted to cut all ties and that she absolved him from any responsibility for the girls. Learning he'd tried to contribute and her mom had refused was a game changer for Cassie. But the part that had tipped the scales in a big way was when she'd learned that while her father was incarcerated, he'd spent his time studying. He'd earned a degree in religious studies and had joined the prison ministry. That and keeping his nose clean had earned him early release.

Now that he was a free man, he continued his mission of counseling inmates to help them see the error of their ways and learn to be contributing members of society when they earned their freedom.

While their relationship hadn't healed completely—that could only be accomplished by trust earned over time—they were on the right track.

Even though Dalton had not included the footage of Ray's surprise visit, Cassie had still reached out and invited him up for the premiere. He had graciously accepted. It warmed Cassie's heart the way the McFadden family had welcomed him with open arms.

But tonight was all about *Selling Sandcastle*.

For the hour-long episode (which ended up being about forty-five minutes sans commercials), the cast and crew had VIP seats up front, and the rest of the town could sit on folding chairs that had been set up, or they could bring their own blanket to lounge on if they chose.

After the show, which Cassie had to admit was pretty darned entertaining and portrayed everyone in a good light, was over, the entire cast, including Gabby, who had volunteered to be Luna's stage handler for the evening, went up onstage for a question-and-answer session moderated by hometown hero Dalton Hart.

This was the part that Cassie was the most nervous about. Even though her sixth sense told her something was afoot, she told herself to be a good sport. If it came down to it and Dalton asked something inappropriate to cause a stir, she didn't have to answer.

Cassie and Logan were seated on the end, and Dalton seemed to be working his way down the line. So they were the last ones to be grilled.

"Cassie and Logan, the two of you met and fell in love on the set of *Selling Sandcastle. Huh? Huh?*" Dalton said.

If he brings up the dog-food dress now, I will throw a chair at him.

Actually, she knew she would grit her teeth and laugh it off, but the chair revenge was fun to think about.

Logan reached out and grabbed her hand. "Yes, we did."

Just the touch of him calmed her. It was like coming home. Even though Tinsley Cove had felt like home for a long time now. Home was anywhere Logan was.

"I know you two kept your relationship on the down low for a while as you figured things out," Dalton said. "And now everyone in town knows you're a couple, but is there anything else you'd like to share about your relationship that we don't already know?"

What an odd question. Like what?

Even though they weren't shy about being a couple, some things were private.

For once Cassie was at a loss for words, and she shot Logan a bemused glance.

"There's one thing I'd like for everyone to know," he said into the microphone.

Then he stood up and pulled Cassie to her feet.

"What's going on, Logan?" she whispered.

Holding her hand, Logan turned to the audience. "This woman changed my life. I know most of you know that I've been through some ups and downs over the years. Some of the lows were very low, but this patient, kind, caring, beautiful woman didn't give up on me."

Pinpricks of joy and gratitude for this man needled her, making her eyes water. She had to take a deep breath and blink a few times to keep the tears from breaching.

"There's only one thing missing." Logan turned to Cassie and fell down on one knee.

Goose bumps broke out over her entire body. Was what she hoped was happening really happening?

The next part—him reaching into the pocket of his tux and pulling out a little blue box—happened in beautiful slow motion. A chorus of gasps rippled through the crowd, and then everyone fell absolutely quiet as if they were holding their collective breath.

"Cassie, will you make me the happiest man in the world and spend the rest of your life with me? Will you marry me?"

Cassie's hands flew to her mouth. She was so choked up with happy tears that she couldn't get the single most important word out of her throat. So she nodded.

As Logan slid a gorgeous, classic round sparkler of a solitaire onto Cassie's finger, her insides tumbled. When Logan pulled her into his arms and the entire town of Tinsley Cove cheered, for the first time in ages, she felt completely whole.

Gabby trotted Luna over to join her family.

As Logan took the leash, Cassie knew she was finally home.

* * * * *

#2965 FOR THE RANCHER'S BABY
Men of the West • by Stella Bagwell

Maggie Malone traveled to Stone Creek Ranch to celebrate her best friend's wedding—not fall in love herself! But ranch foreman Cordell Hollister is too charming and handsome to resist! When their fling ends with a pregnancy, will a marriage of convenience be enough for the besotted bride-to-be?

#2966 HOMETOWN REUNION
Bravo Family Ties • by Christine Rimmer

Sixteen years ago, Hunter Bartley left town to seek fame and fortune. Now the TV star is back, eager to reconnect with the woman he left behind...and the love he could never forget. But can JoBeth Bravo trust love a second time when she won't leave and he can never stay?

#2967 WINNING HER FORTUNE
The Fortunes of Texas: Hitting the Jackpot • by Heatherly Bell

Alana Searle's plan for one last hurrah before her secret pregnancy is exposed has gone awry! Her winning bachelor-auction date is *not* with one of the straitlaced Maloney brothers but with bad boy Cooper Fortune Maloney himself. What if her unexpected valentine is daddy material after all?

#2968 THE LAWMAN'S SURPRISE
Top Dog Dude Ranch • by Catherine Mann

Charlotte Pace is already overwhelmed with her massive landscaping job and caring for her teenage brother. Having Sheriff Declan Winslow's baby is just *too much*! But Declan isn't ready to let the stubborn, independent beauty forget their fling...nor the future they could have together.

#2969 SECOND TAKE AT LOVE
Small Town Secrets • by Nina Crespo

Widow Myles Alexander wants to renovate and sell his late wife's farmhouse—not be the subject of a Hollywood documentary. But down-to-earth director Holland Ainsley evokes long-buried feelings, and soon he questions everything he thought love could be. Until drama follows her to town, threatening to ruin everything...

#2970 THE BEST MAN'S PROBLEM
The Navarros • by Sera Taíno

Rafael Navarro thrives on routines and control. Until his sister recruits him to help best man Etienne Galois with her upcoming nuptials. Spontaneous and adventurous, Etienne seems custom-made to trigger Rafi's annoyance...and attraction. Can he face his surfacing feelings before their wedding partnership ends in disaster?

HARLEQUIN
PLUS

Try the best multimedia subscription service for romance readers like you!

Read, Watch and Play.

Experience the easiest way to get the romance content you crave.

Start your **FREE TRIAL** at
www.harlequinplus.com/freetrial.